D1882220

the soul game

how fair or unfair?

RICHA AGARWAL
SUNIL PRAKASH

Vani Book Company

Vani Book Company
Head Office

4695, 21-A, Daryaganj, New Delhi 110 002, India
Phone : +91 11 23273167 Fax : +91 11 23275710

Registered Bookstores and Offices

Ashok Rajpath, Patna 800 004, Bihar
Coffee House Campus, Mahatma Gandhi Marg, Allahabad 211 001, Uttar Pradesh
Mahatma Gandhi International Hindi University, Wardha 442 001, Maharashtra
Sultania Road, Motia Park, Bhopal 462 001, Madhya Pradesh
Goripur Taliya Para, 313, R.B.C. Road 24- Parganas (North) Kolkata 743 166, West Bengal

www.vaniprakashan.com
marketing@vaniprakashan.in
sales@vaniprakashan.in

THE SOUL GAME
by Richa Agarwal, Sunil Prakash

ISBN : 978-93-89563-23-8
Non-Fiction

© Richa Agarwal, Sunil Prakash
First Edition 2019

Price : ₹ 199 $ 9.99 £ 5.99

The Soul Game is published by Vani Book Company, an imprint of Vani Prakashan Group copyrighted in 2019 to *Richa Agarwal* and *Sunil Prakash.* All rights reserved. No part of this book may be reproduced, in any form by any machanical or electronic means (including photocopying, recording or information storage or reprinted) without permission in writing from publisher. Users are not allowed to mount this file on any network servers including e-mail.

Printed and bound in India at Jayant Printery, LLP, Mumbai-02

Vani Prakashan's signature motif is created by Artist Maqbool Fida Husain

Dedication

To the biggest divine presence in my life—my parents Mr. R.P. Agarwal & Mrs. Bimla Agarwal who have always believed in me and raised me into a loving, compassionate & confident human being. To my loving husband Gyan who has always encouraged me to chase my dreams, to all my sisters for always standing by me in my most difficult times, to all my nephews & nieces to make my life fulfilling and last but not the least, to my little angel, my daughter Anvi, who brought me into this beautiful field of spirituality, healing and empathy as soon as she was born. Also, to every person who has played an important role in the execution of this book.

Richa Agarwal

This Book is dedicated to my lovely wife Anju and children who always believe in me, Reena my associate for all the support she provided me with this book, to all my friends, students, clients and to all those people who are doing their best to make our world a better place to live.

Sunil Prakash

Foreword

Here is a book dealing with subject of soul, rebirth, Karma and destiny but it is not your regular religious or even spiritual book. Far from it, the book has a thorough scientific tone, no doubt coming from a person of science. The book deals with questions that perhaps have disturbed every thinking mind at point. The book rids the concepts like Soul, Karma and Rebirth of all the religious stigma attached with them and analyses those in a scientific format.

I was most intrigued to learn that our soul is keeping record of our actions in this birth and maybe even previous ones and all these records could shape our coming rebirths. This is exactly what this book proposes to address, a simple assessment and explanation to the one of the most complex questions of the journey of our soul and how can we analyse it.

The book presents a fresh and unique perspective to our present and past lives. Where good and bad Karmas that affects your next life is being treated as profit and losses and just Like a company's books need to show profits, good entrepreneur, one needs to have of good Karma than bad Karma. Sanskrit saying, "Yatha Pinde Tatha Brahmande", which means As is microcosm so is macrocosm - As is human so is cosmos, fits aptly to describe this book.

When I was requested to write a foreword for a book with the name, *The Soul Game,* I hesitated due to my limited orientation into the complex realms of spirituality- whether spiritual science or the deep philosophy behind it. But this book is a perfect guide for anyone who wishes to understand more about our soul's journey written in the most relatable manner. This book is an ideal blend of science, spirituality and philosophy on an issue that is very often misunderstood by most of us.

Not just the journey of a Soul, this book also elaborates on the journey of the Human Body that is attached ot it-through all its phases of Life, Death and after-death. Though this book, I learnt more about the "mind" of the soul and how it finds its outlet; and how the soul has its own set of desires that it wishes to fulfil several actions. Amidst this unique and powerful journey, the Human Body is nothing more than a vehicle but to fulfil these desires and aspirations of the Soul.

We, humans, don't get to choose much that happens in our life, it is someone else who chooses for us and we act like those AI robots we see these days, just enacting the role that has been created for them. An invaluable and compassionate harvest of eternal insights that will both excite and challenge the reader. *The Soul Game* is a powerful book and I would like to recommend it to those who are seeking answers on our existence and challenge the pre-conceived notions the society has set.

Gaurie Dwivedi
Economist
Executive Editor – News X
Columnist – Sunday Guardian
Ex-Economic Times (Sr. Journalist)
Ex-Times Now (Sr. Editor)
World Renowned Classical Dancer

Testimonials

Prof. Dr. Vivek Gupta

MD, DM, FACC, FESC, FSCAI, FEAPCI, FAPSIC, FICC, FIC (FRANCE) FCSI, FIEIC, FIMSA
Senior Interventional Cardiologist
Fellow, American College of Cardiology
Fellow, European Society of Cardiology
Fellow, Society of Cardiovascular Angiography and Intervention
Fellow of Cardiology Cardiological Society of India
Fellow, European Association of Percutaneous Coronary Interventions
Fellow, Asia Pacific Society of Interventional Cardiology
Fellow, Society of Cardiac Catheterization and Interventions
Fellow, Indian College of Cardiology
Fellow, Indo European Intervention Council
Formerly Fellow in Interventional Cardiology (Rouen, France)

Apollo Hospitals HEART INSTITUTES

Accredited by Joint Commission International

"Medicines can cure diseases, but only doctors can cure patients" – Carl Jung

This is a famous quote by Carl Jung, a very famous Swiss psychiatrist and psychoanalyst who founded analytical psychology. The meaning of this quote is deep. Having been practicing as a cardiologist for so many years, I truly and faithfully believe in the extreme power of our mind in curing ourselves as well as having the will in curing others.

I firmly believe that being a doctor does not only mean prescribing the right medicines, but also developing an empathic connect with the patient heart to heart so as to create a conducive environment in their mind for healing.

This book "The Soul Game" also helps us get in touch with that divine power of the human mind which can lead to happiness, healing as well as suffering of a human body. There are so many patients who have never had any history of cardiac issues in their family but suddenly suffer from something like a cardiac arrest and then there are those who have history of cardiac issues running in their family but never themselves face any cardiac problem. I always felt this is related to our karmas in one or the other way.

Then I came across this book "The Soul Game" and my belief was reaffirmed. It explains the Karma theory so beautifully and the journey of a soul through life. Its fascinating how a Soul lays down its entire plan of how it would realise its purpose and fulfil it's goals through a human body in the next life.

I have been a believer of Past Life and reincarnation and the proposition suggested in this book about how our karmas, past lives and life situations are all related is beautiful.

I would surely recommend this book to the medical fraternity so that we medical professionals can also try and see the other side of the coin.

24/10/19

India's First Internationally Accredited Hospital

Sarita Vihar, Delhi - Mathura Road, New Delhi - 76 (India) **Tel. :** 29871034, 26925858 **Fax :** 011-26825631
Cardiology OPD Block Room # 1034, Extn. 1034
Timings : Mon, Wed. & Fri. (1 p.m. to 5 p.m.), Tue, Thus & Sat (9 a.m. to 1 p.m.)
M. I. Clinic : C-36, Sarita Vihar, New Delhi - 110076, **Ph. :** 011-26952758 **Mob. :** +91-9810108440, 9810108445
E-mail : cardiologistvivekgupta@gmail.com mlgvivek@hotmail.com **Website :** www.iecr.in www.apollohospdelhi.com
Contact Secretary : 9560214864, 9560895509

FS 526454 EMS 526455

ISO 9001 003 ISO 14001 003

RAJIV GANDHI CANCER INSTITUTE AND RESEARCH CENTRE

Dr. Ullas Batra
MD, DM(Medical Oncology), ECMO, FAGE
Chief of Thoracic Medical Oncology
In Charge, Med Unit-V

SECTOR-V, ROHINI, DELHI-110 085
Tel.: 91-11-47022264
Mobile : 97110-80001
Fax : 2705-1037
E-mail : ullasbatra@gmail.com

Dated : 23-10-2019

In my long career as an Oncologist, I've come across a plethora of very agonizing cases of cancer patients that it has made me question time and again the very existence of any "divine power". I used to wonder so many times, whether any such supreme power or God or whatsoever we may call it, even exists? If it does, why do people go through such merciless torture and suffering in the hands of nature?

At the same time, even in our Medical Profession, there are times when we see miracles happening. Patients who have lost all hope recover in a rather miraculous manner. This kind of reaffirmed the existence of a greater force.

This book, "The Soul Game" has convincingly answered many of such questions of mine. It provides the readers with a clear perspective about the theory of Karma, the Soul, the Mind, the Body and the role of almighty. It also explains how we suffer due to our own actions or Karmas, and not due to the wishes of God, that too in a very rational manner.

The case studies given in the book are eye opening and intriguing. I sincerely feel this book will enlighten readers to a great extent in regard to the journey of our Soul, the human sufferings and the reasons behind them.

It's a great piece of work compiled with a lot of effort and experience. Readers will surely appreciate the answers it provides to the problems being faced in life.

A must read !

Dr. ULLAS BATRA
MD, DM (Medical Oncology), ECMO, FAGE
Rajiv Gandhi Cancer Institute & Research Centre
Sector-V, Rohini, Delhi-110085
Regd. No. DMC-24258

DR. ULLAS BATRA
MD, DM, FAGE, ECMO
Sr. Consultant & Unit InCharge
DMC No. 24258

Justice Deepak Verma
Former Judge
Supreme Court of India

Testimonial for "The Soul Game"

A daring and should I say, "blasphemous" attempt to scientifically explain the soul-body relationship. Blasphemous in the sense that it presents a postulation that defies the doctrines of almost all the major religions.

I also rate this book very highly for rationally explaining what the Law of Karma is and how it functions. The functioning of the Law of Karma is not very different from our Judicial law. However one major difference between the two is that while judicial law only mete out punishment for the criminal actions, the Law of Karma also rewards the good or positive actions of a person. There are ample literature available for those who want to learn Judicial law. But for The Law of Karma, this is one of the best works, which would appeal to rational and scientific minded people. In present day life, it is necessary to learn and know about the soul, which is likely to improve our "Karmas" during this life time, to achieve true and contended life.

Wishing the Writer M/s Richa Agarwal greater success in life and career, to reach the zenith.

22.10.2019

Justice Deepak Verma
Former Judge, Supreme Court of India

Office: D-19, Third Floor, Geetanjali Enclave, New Delhi - 110017
Residence: A-16, Second Floor, Geetanjali Enclave, New Delhi - 110017
T: 011 41064992 | **M:** +91 9717393521 | +91 9301538508 | **E:** justicedverma@gmail.com

SANJIV SEN
Senior Advocate
Supreme Court of India

I'm falling short of words to explain how thrilled, excited and fascinated I am by the theory and cases given in this book. "The Soul Game" seems to me like an encyclopaedia which enlightens is about Soul, Mind, Body and The Law Of Karma. Being a lawyer professionally, I find the language of law instantly and though "The Soul Game" is all about meta-physical stuff, the theory of Karma being explained in the language of law enamours me.

Exceptional is the word for this book.

SANJIV SEN

H-4, FF, Kailash Colony, New Delhi – 110 048
Phone: 011- 41708686
E-mail: sanjivsenoffice@gmail.com

Apollo International Limited

I absolutely loved this book "The Soul Game". It is an eye-opener and gives an altogether different perspective to the theory of the Soul as compared to the traditional theory. I feel deeply enlightened as this book has made me question a lot of ideas which got imbibed in my mind due to my Belief System. The book also resonates with the thinking of a scientific mind and reinforces that everything can be conquered through science.

I have known Richa personally for almost 2 decades, she was a contributor in one of my previous ventures. Though she was very young at that time, I always felt she had a spiritual bent of mind. It was really not a surprise for me to come to know that she switched careers by 180 degree, from being a Programme Management Professional to a Hypnotherapist. Looking at this piece of work by her, I must say that she has deep understanding of the subject and "The Soul Game" is a brilliant piece of work. The cover itself compelled me to get into the details of the book.

I would surely like to recommend this "brilliant piece of work" to everyone irrespective of their background, age, culture and interests.

Raaja Kanwar
Managing Director
Apollo International Limited

Corporate Office: Apollo Towers, Plot No. 20, Sector 44, Gurgaon-122 002, Haryana, INDIA
Registered Office: Office No. 303, Third Floor, DLF Courtyard, Saket, New Delhi - 110 017
T: +91 124 6740 200, F: +91 124 4197 222, E: info@apolloindia.com
CIN - U74899DL1994PLC061080, www.apolloindia.com

pwc

This book "The Soul Game" is truly remarkable as it brings to light a lot of facts which we as humans never think of. It is shocking to discover how we human bodies are at the behest of the Mind and the Soul. I had personally never thought of this theory in this manner. It is indeed "mind-blowing" to discover the facts outlined in this book and makes us question a lot of things! The concept of this book is very unique and compels a person to take some time out and think deeper. The book cover itself is very interesting and mysterious!

I would like to recommend this book highly to each and every person as it would create a lot of difference in the way we have been thinking about the Soul so far!

Praveen Bhambani
Partner

PricewaterhouseCoopers Pvt. Ltd., Building No. 10, 17th Floor, Tower - C, DLF Cyber City, Gurgaon - 122 002
T: +91 (124) 3306000, F: +91 (124) 3306999, www.pwc.com/india

CIN : U74140WB1983PTC036093
Registered Office : Plot No. Y-14, Block EP, Sector V, Salt Lake, Kolkata 700 091

Testimonial for the Book "The Soul Game"

I have been a Founder Employee of CNN NEWS18 and have been working with the group for over 14 years now. In total, 15+ years of work ex in "chasing headlines"– both in print as well as electronic. During all these years, I have met different sorts of people, seen different kinds of situations arising in the world, I wonder we all go through so much thick and thin in life – be it people or places. Even places go through difficult times. This many a times made me think why all this happens? Why at one instance a person is happy and right at the next instance something may happen that makes a person sad? When Richa gave me this book, I was intrigued looking at the attractive book cover. Little did I know that this book would give me answers to so many questions making rounds in my mind all the time. I have gathered a lot of knowledge after reading this book specially the cases given in this book are mind-blowing. I am very thankful to Richa for sharing "The Soul Game" with me and I would recommend it to everyone.

Anita Sinha

Senior Journalist

Network 18

Acknowledgement

Foremost, to all our clients who have helped us gain this knowledge which enabled and empowered us to write this book.

The idea of this book has been brewing in our mind for around a decade and perhaps from the time we started our practice as Clinical Hypnotherapists. So all along, each and every experience, while teaching Hypnotherapy to our students or while putting a client into trance for therapy, was going into developing this book.

Also, a big thank you to our Publisher & Editor Aditi Maheshwari for understanding the importance of this subject and giving us the opportunity to share our thoughts with the masses. Also to her constant guidance, encouragement and patience, without which, this book wouldn't have been possible.

We would also like to thank each and every person who has been instrumental in the production of this book including the designers, printers and all other people who have helped us in anyway during all stages of this book. Thank you to each and every person who took the time out of their busy schedules to read the manuscript and provide testimonies to further motivate and encourage us.

A very big thank you to our family members for always being there to support us at every turn in life.

Last, but not the least, we deeply acknowledge the Creator for its divine presence and guidance every moment of our life.

Richa Agarwal
Sunil Prakash

Preface

We all understand *Life* as a combination of three things : *Body, Mind* and *Soul.* What if we are told that our life is not lesser than a Balance Sheet? Well yes, you must have heard this analogy from many people. However, this time it's a little different.

This Balance Sheet spans across multiple lifetimes, rather than constricting itself to only one Life. Each lifetime is like a year's account book. The ledger of this lifetime keeps and maintains an account of all good and bad deeds.

Each of these account books (lifetimes) have assets & liabilities, profits and loss, debtors and creditors.

Why do we want this entire *system* of *Life* to be so complicated? Who has made it so complicated? Who is the culprit-our *Body* or is it our *Mind?*

The answer is *no*! It is all the game plan of our Soul. Our Soul is the *entity*, which has made this entire system very complicated for its own selfish motive of not losing its importance in humanity.

The Soul uses Body's each and every cell, atoms, molecules, tissues, muscles, organs, bones, lymph, systems, nerves, brain, hormones, minerals, metals, chemicals, air etc., just to fulfill its desires whether good or bad, satisfy its emotions, makes life simple or traumatic. Finally at the time of Death, it forgets the Body and leaves it lifeless.

Based on the data collected during the last life journey and the previous lives, the Soul consults its balance sheet from the Mind Entity and then decides the next move.

In this book, for the first time, we will indulge into these Soul's Games to uncover the selfish motives of the Soul and discover, how we, as human bodies are entangled thoroughly and deeply into the web designed by the Soul, which offers no escape.

Contents

Chapter One

The Soul : Our Accountant

There is a big anomaly in our Minds and we all have made an effort to unwind lot of myths about is there anything called Soul and if so, where does it exist and what is the game it is trying to play with us? To understand what the Soul is and why we call it our accountant, let us first understand how its evolution happened on earth.

Science : The findings of science may be relevant to one'sunderstanding of the Soul depending on one's belief regarding the relationship between the Soul and the Mind. One problem with seeking scientific evidence for the Soul is that there is no clear or unique definition of what the Soul is.

Parapsychology : Some parapsychologists have attempted to establish by scientific experiments whether a Soul is separate from the brain, as more commonly defined in religion rather than as a synonym of psyche or Mind, exists.

To understand the existence of the Soul in our world, it is imperative to first learn about how our world, our universe came into existence.

The Big Bang Theory : According to English astronomer

Fred Hoyle, our Universe came into existence through the Big Bang. Have you ever heard about what the Big Bang Theory and what it led to?

It is one of the several scientific models that attempts to explain why the Universe is the way it is.Big Bang Theory is one of the most accepted theory by the vast majority of physicists on the origin of the Universe.

Fred Hoyle coined the term *Big Bang* while explaining about the formation of our universe, during a 1949 BBC radio broadcast, saying : *"These theories were based on the hypothesis that all the matter in the universe was created in one big bang at a particular time in the remote past"*. The Big Bang Theory describes the 'birth' and 'development' of the Universe from the time just after it came into existence up to today.

Have you ever wondered who was behind the creation of this magnificent Universe? Scientist around the world are still working on to establish the power or source behind this development, but there are a lot of common views between the different sources such as ourclairvoyants, psychics, other gifted people and our general believe system.

According to them, one thing is common-there is some supreme power which is the primary source of the universal energy and the master mind behind all this development. In this book, for our understanding, hereafter we will call this supreme power as the "creator".

The Soul or our accountant came into existence through the Big Bang. It was rather sent by the "Creator" to help evolve life, support it and keep it protected since future growth was envisaged on the Earth and to monitor all this it was important to develop an energetic connection between the Earth and the universe, so the "Creator" created an entity called the "Soul".

The Soul had to go through the following transitions before finally entering the Human body—

1. Crystal Age
2. Plant Age
3. Animal Age

Let us read about this journey of the Soul in more details-

THE CRYSTAL AGE

Millions and millions of years back 'The Big Bang' happened, various galaxies were formed, and each galaxy had its own planets around it. From this came up the EARTH, which was in the form of molten liquid which cooled slowly to form the Earth's crust in the form of minerals, metals and dust.

The upper crust cooled and became heavy. This exerted heavy pressure on the lower crust. With high temperature and pressure it took various shapes and formed different elements and heterogeneous substances. This resulted in crystal formation of various shapes, sizes, elements, metals and minerals.

The Soul was empowered by the "Creator" with some unique powers and then sent to enter into Crystals. This inhabitance had a purpose and responsibility which was to develop an energetic connection between the Earth and the universe and to energize the Crystals for further growth and development

Since then Crystals have special powers and energies, which they emit out in the universe. On the instructions from the Creator, the crystals thus provided this energy and information to the universe in the form of light, electrical energy, magnetic energy, through the geometrical constellations and the other galaxies and planets. This energy could also be used in healing of the plants, animals and humans, which we will be discussing later.

Eventually all this power and position made the Soul very arrogant and it wanted to be free from all activities, so it created another energy entity, called the "Mind", and assigned it the work of maintaining a data base about what the Crystals are going through and what was happening around in the universe.

With all the good, came the shortcomings- the feeling of being 'Trapped',sincethere was no release for further evolution. The Soul and the Mind felt trapped since they were confined deep inside of the crystal, which was hard, stationary, and embedded deep inside in the earth's core, surrounded by, heat and gaseous fumes. The only life was the pulsating movements of energies inside the hard rocks, which were either in the form of dust or stones. If the crystals were lying on the earth's surface, they had to face the coldest of the weather, drenched in rains, bear the heat of the sun, and the heat from the earth's beneath. However, they could not do anything as were unable to move and had to silently bear the brunt of the environment. The Crystal felt now nothing further was left to explore.

There was no growth, only deterioration, life was long, very long and that too for millions of years.So the Crystal persistently requested to the Creator-that 'I' am trapped and need to live and experience more meaningful and dynamic life, the Creator also felt the need to evolve something new, so it evolved something which was more mobile. The Creator evolved the plants on the surface of the earth, and the Soul through the plants tried to achieve some mobility. Whether it was a success or a failure, is to be seen next.

THE PLANT AGE

On the request of the Soul who was feeling entrapped inside the Crystal, the creator created a single CELL that was mobile. Placed the consciousness into this cell to seek more experiences. This cell was the cell of Algae. From one single cell, they transformed themselves to the tallest trees. The evolution and growth continued, as it was an open world, with lots of free space, time, feelings & energies. The Souls of the plants evolved into intelligent forms of life that showed a will to survive, thrive and interact. Plant showed intelligence, intent, sensitivity to feel and touch, grow, react, and multiply, varied expectancy of life from days to years.

They developed the sense of beauty in structure, color and aroma. They could bend, grow in consonance with nature, and seek support. They developed the state of male-female differentiation and the growth of progeny. Nevertheless, it got dependent on nature. It is through the seed system, which when falls on earth, will only grow.

Thus we can say that the progress was much more to what it was in Crystal age, but then fell back in the following :

- Power to fight back with environment and diseases.
- Lack of mobility, have to complete their life at one place only.
- Survival, growth and progeny totally dependent on nature and other resources such as-climate, soil, water, wind etc.

When you get some, you start looking for more, so the Soul felt trapped inside the plants as there was no mobility and the stationary life was now becoming very boring. For their very existence and progeny they had to depend on the nature.

The Soul again approached the Creator and placed their need to evolve a new species to whom more of mobility, emotions and power is available. Thus, on request, the Creator evolved the animals.

THE ANIMAL AGE

Animals are highly evolved creatures with lots of unique features. They are mobile, can move from one place to another.

Their sense of touch, sound and smell is far more developed from the plants. They have evolved into many different forms of bodies. From a single cell animal called Amoeba to high and strong creatures like Lion, Rhino, and Elephants etc. Animals have group Souls, one for each species or subspecies.

Developed the reproductive system for growth in population. Does not have to fully depend on the nature. Lives in groups and have the concept of Male & Female. Developed the sense of love, caring, sensitivity and self-healing. Have evolved in millions of bodies like structures.

They developed the high sense of vision and frequency to detect even at night. Highly adapted to ultrasonic waves and could sense dangers well in advance to move to more secure places.There was a fast and deep evolution from the Plants to the Animals. Some of the unique features animals exhibited are—

- Multibody
- Deep sense of smell, taste, vision
- Hard working
- Loving, caring and concerted feeling towards their group members.
- Different varieties of animals helped in growth and pollination in plants. Plants were, totally dependent on nature and animals for growth in progeny.

- Carbon dioxide released by the animals helped the plants for their living and oxygen released by plants helped animals to survive.

The Souls had to do lot of experiments with animal bodies and to adapt in all form of environments, from land, waterto air. For food they were self-dependent and had to fetch, thus adapt to nature or restrict their dwelling according to the availability of food. Highly insecure, thus lived in groups. Had to be satisfied with whatever is available.

Moreover, an individual animal cannot exit the Group Soul, the Soul of its species and so, it was not possible to begin as an individual Soul, living life on its own terms, with its own journey, personality and experiences.

This made life of the Soul sedentary and monotonous. Soul had to face hundreds of groups, types, shapes, both short lived from hours to long years of life. This again initiated for another evolution. An evolution where mobility increased, and EGO was brought in. A sense of competition, 'I" and "ME" were brought in. Mammals were evolved from animals. They were called Humans.

THE HUMAN AGE

Again a revolutionary change was brought in. All different bodies were reduced to only two physical genders, one of masculine called Male and another of feminine Called Female. This was done with the idea to bring unison amongthe human beings to live life peacefully, progressively, harmoniously and compassionately. There was less of work in terms of the different forms of bodies to be maintained so the Creator decided to make this single human Body to have more facilities such as movement, , vision, sense of touch, feel, smell, hear

& taste. With all this one more important sense, "sense of spirituality" was also inculcated.

With so much to do, the following had to be reduced—

- Speed & energies
- The sense of far and advanced warnings
- Ultrasonic information
- Night vision

Becoming dependent, made the humans to develop new ideas, which resulted into increased brain size, the brain cells evolved faster than any other part of body. This resulted in less of hard work and more of dependency in the development of the physical body, which became big, and more flexible to do more new things.

Here came the evolution with change in 'Body' to 'change in the Thoughts'. The above changes were made by the Creator with the good intention to promote homogeneity in the human beings. The life started with this thought, when the Adam and Eve were sent to this planet Earth. The life was carefree and peaceful, but the Soul did not find it interesting.

Soon Eve ate the fruit from the "forbidden tree"(The Tree of the Knowledge of Good and Evil) and shared some with Adam, - the sense of Cruelty, ID, EGO, I and ME all were brought in and it became the world of rules, laws, survival, competition, and showoff. The Soul wanted to see what happens when all these ills are brought in the life of the Humans.

Spirituality

For the Soul, the rules of embodiment, experimenting and then discarding the body (at the time of death) are the same whether it is a crystal, plant, animal or human.

Since everything is alive in universe, whether it is an atom, a crystal, a plant, an animal or a humaneverything has some level of consciousness, The difference of vibration of each level goes with the level of complexity of each kingdom, 1) mineral kingdom - 1st dimension vibration, lowest complexity 2) plant kingdom - 2nd dimension vibration, higher complexity, 3) animal (including humans) kingdom - 3rd dimension vibration, highest complexity as far as humanity knows now. So everything has a "soul" it's a just a question of how high or low the consciousness is.

Spiritualty has never been a point of study when we discussed the Crystal age, Plant age or Animal age, but became important when we talk about the Soul of Human age.

For the question : *Is there anything called Soul and if sowhere does it exist in the human being?*

The answer is-The Soul is our consciousness. Our consciousness is energy, which has no form or location. This energy is part of the whole universe. This consciousness which we have termed as God, Soul or Metaphysical Energy.

The meaning of life is to evolve our consciences to higher consciousness, which is the source of all existence, the formation of the Universe, the planets, solar system and even our consciousness.

It is considered by various schools of thoughts that the Soul of an individual is located in the heart. It is not visible to human eyes. It is the secret of the Creator and so it is invisible. Feelings are because of the presence of the Soul in our Body. The Body stops functioning (death) when the Soul leaves the Body.

The "Soul" is a series of electrical impulses. When we die, these impulses flow to the Universe to rejoin the universal energy. Soul belongs to the Creator and it should return to the Creator in that form in which it came.

This gave birth to a popular philosophical explanation for the existence of GOD and SOUL. Therefore, it is accepted with all the sects that GOD exists and we need not go into the details of its existence.

Let us understand what is this Energy or Consciousness we have just discovered and what role it has to play in our lives.

GOD – SOUL – CONSCIOUSNESS. For practical purpose and further discussions, let us refer all to be SOUL.

The "Soul", in many religious, philosophical and mythological traditions is immortal essence of a living being. According to most of the Abrahamic religions, immortal Souls belong only to human beings. For example, the Catholic theologian Thomas attributed "Soul" (anima) to all organisms but argued that only human Souls are immortal. Other religions (most notably Jainism and Hinduism) teach that all biological organisms have Souls, and others teach that even non-biological entities (such as rivers and mountains) possess Souls.

Other Views :

Egyptian Religion : In the ancient Egyptian religion, anindividual was believed to be made up of various elements, some physical and some spiritual.

Bahai : It states that the Soul is immortal and continues tolive after the physical death of the human Body. Heaven can be seen partly as the Soul's state of nearness to God and hell as a state of remoteness from God.

Buddhism : Teaches that all things are in a constant stateof flux; all is changing, and no permanent state exists by itself. Only consciousness continue to exist even after death.

Christianity : According to a common Christian Eschatology, when people die, their Souls will be judged by God and determined to go to Heaven or to Gahanna. Reference to the fact that the spirit or the Soul is separate from the Body or the physical form, can also be found in The Holy Bible -

Reference : Ecclesiastes 12:7

And the dust returns to the earth as it was, and the spirit returns to God who gave it.

Islam : Reference to the "Soul" can also be found in the Qur'an

> **"I created you from one Soul, and from the Soul. I created its mate so that you may live in harmony and love."**

Jainism : In Jainism every living being, from a bacteriumto human, has a Soul. Till the time the Soul is not liberated from the innumerable Birth and Death cycle, it gets attached to a particular Body based on its Karmas.The Soul lives its ownlife, not for the purpose of the Body, but the Body lives for the purpose of the Soul.

Hinduism : In Hinduism, the Sanskrit words most closelycorresponding to Soul are jiva, 'Ātman' and 'purusha', meaning the individual self.

The three major schools of Hindu philosophy agree that the 'Atman' (individual self) is related to 'Brahman' or the 'Paramatman', the Supreme Self. The atman becomes involved in the process of becoming and transmigrating through cycles of birth and death because of ignorance of its own true nature.

The spiritual path consists of self-realization and returning to the source which is Brahma.

In Bhagavad Gita 2.20 Lord Krishna describes the atman in the following way :

Bhagvad Gita - Chapter 2, verse 20

> **"najayatemriyatevakadacin 'nayambhutvabhavitava nabhuyah'ajonityahsasvato yam purano'nahanyateh anyamanesarire"**

Verse Translation :

For the Soul there is neither birth nor death at any time. He has not come into being, does not come into being, and will not come into being. He is unborn,eternal, ever – existing and primeval. He is not slain when the Body is slain.

When the Atman (Soul) becomes embodied it is called 'birth', when the Atman leaves a Body it is called 'death'. The Atman transmigrates from one Body to another Body based on karmic [performed deeds] reactions. Brahma is regarded as the creator of this universe, according to the Hindu philosophy, which is considered to be the oldest, space and time are considered to be Maya (illusion).

Bhagvad Gita - Chapter 2, verse 22

> **"Vasamsijirnaniyathavihayanavanigrhnatinaro, paranitathasariranivihayajirnanyanyanaisamyatinavani"**

Verse Translation :

As a human being puts on a new garments, giving up old ones, the Soul similarly accepts new material bodies, giving up the old and useless one.

(When the Soul takes a new material Body, why does it not take a new Mind, minus the memories of past lives? Is again not a Soul's game to torture the Body?)

Bhagvad Gita - Chapter 2, verse 24

> **"acchedyo 'yamadahyo' yamakledya 'sosyaeva ca, nityahsarva-gatahsthanuracalo' yamsanatanah"**

Verse Translation :

The Soul is indestructible; the Soul is incombustible, insoluble and unwitherable. The Soul is eternal, all pervasive, unmodifiable, immovable and primordial. The Soul on one hand has made itself strong, powerful, indestructible and invincible and on the other hand made the Body very weak, vulnerable and fragile.

According to the Vedas to enjoy variety of experiences, the Soul takes incarnation in over 8,400,000 kinds of different Bodies. Moreover although we dwell within the Body, the Soul is the actual owner and controller of the Body. It is the Soul who decides when to enter or leave the Body. When the Soul leaves the Body, the Body disintegrates and the person is declared dead.

So by we now understand that the Soul who is acting as the accountant of our life came into existence through the Big Bang Theory. It was rather sent by the "Creator" to help evolve life, keep it protected and support it. However over the ages, the Soul began to feel that it is losing its importance and started gaining more and more control on the Body and the Mind.

The evolution journey of the Soul started from the Crystal Age to the Plant Age, Animal Age and finally into Human Age. Once it attained the Human form, which is an amalgamation of all sensory inputs and outputs, physical body to experience worldly desires and unique ability to feel and express emotional information, through various communication abilities, it began to call its shots.

Like an accountant, it started making an account of every experience a human goes through, based on this, it initiated an altogether a new theory called "The Theory of Karma."

Chapter two

The Karma Theory

DEBTORS & CREDITORS

In the balance sheet of life, Karmas are our debts that we owe to others and credits that we have earned. The way Karma Theory has been designed again makes us fall prey into the hands of the Soul. Karma, Reincarnation or Rebirth are most talked about in our scriptures and different Religious mythologies. We need to establish how and why Karma exists and then what are the benefits and pitfalls/ drawbacks, the Body has to bear at the behest of Soul in the name of Karma.

CASE OF HATRED BETWEEN SIBLINGS

A young man around twenty one came with a pressing issue of zero compatibility with his younger brother. The hatred and animosity between them had increasing by the day and now they could not see each other eye to eye. He is always under fear that his younger brother who is just around 17 would kill him. If at home he always kepts the door of his room locked from inside. He did not feel safe in his own home.

After taking his case history, we could not rule a single reason that could justify this degree of hatred and animosity between the siblings. So we decided to do a past life regression session with them.

Once in deep trance, the elder brother went into a past life, where he was a strong and powerful king and in a fit of anger, with his sword brutally killed an innocent, helpless, new born baby.

Now this baby come back in this lifetime as his younger brother to take his revenge and square out the Karmas.

WHAT IS KARMA?

Have you ever found yourself stuck in a situation that feels like a trap? A situation from which you want to run away, but you don't or you can't for a number of reasons and sometimes ever for no reasons. You tend to become irritated, angry and aggressive over trivial issues which hold no importance. A lot of times, in spite of having a great career, a happy family and everything one can wish for, you do not feel happy, you feel low and uncomfortable as if something is missing. At times, you try very hard to take charge of a situation but after a point of time, you ultimately become helpless and the situation takes charge of your life. You always crave for happiness and don't understand how you may find it.

This continues and sooner or later you fall prey to physical diseases, depression, addiction or your relationships start breaking.

Some of these thoughts may be coming over and over again to you—

- I have never harmed anyone in life, why is this happening with me?
- Why am I being humiliated over and over again?

- Why am I incurring financial losses all the time?
- In spite of being so talented, why am I failing at every junction?
- Why do I always attract the wrong people in my life?
- Why there is no physical intimacy between me and my partner?
- Why is that person so happy and I am not, though we are in the same situation?
- Why things do not fall at the right place in spite of my best efforts?
- Why is my child so difficult?
- Why is my relationship with my parents or siblings so rough?
- Why was my child born with physical or mental disabilities?

And so on....

SO WHAT EXACTLY IS KARMA?

The word Karma means action, work or deed. It also refers to the principle of Causation where intent and actions of an individual influence the future of that individual. It is everything that one thinks, feels and does that gets recorded in our cosmic hard-drive i.e. our Mind and thus becomes our permanent Karmic data.

Karma is our actions from our current or past existences, which have resulted in our present state of being. Our life today is a reflection of our past deeds. Good intents and good deeds which are our Credits, contribute to good Karma and future happiness, while bad intents and bad deeds which are our bad debts contribute to bad Karma and future suffering. It is a rule by which the universe balances itself. Our past existences refer to our past incarnations.

A common theme to be observed in the theory of Karma in Hindu, Jain and Buddhist preaching. All actions have consequences which will affect the doer of the action at some future times (the Law of Universal Causation).

One of the earliest association of Karma to the principle of Causation occurs in the "Brihadaranyaka Upanishad", 7th Century of Hinduism. For example—

> **sa vā ayamātmā brahma vijñānamayo manomayaḥ prāṇamayaścakśurmayaḥ śrotramayaḥ pṛthivīmaya āpomayo vāyumaya ākāśamayastejomayo' tejomayaḥ kāmamayo' kāmamayaḥ krodhamayo' krodhamayo dharmamayo' dharmamayaḥ sarvamayastadyadetadidaṃmayo' domaya iti; yathākārī yathācārī tathā bhavati—sādhukārī sādhurbhavati, pāpakārī pāpo bhavati; puṇyaḥ puṇyena karmaṇā bhavati, pāpaḥ pāpena | atho khalvāhuḥ kāmamaya evāyaṃ puruṣa iti; sa yathākāmo bhavati tatkraturbhavati, yatkraturbhavati tatkarma kurute, yatkarma kurute tadabhisaṃpadyate || 5 ||**

That self is indeed Brahman, as well as identified with the intellect, the Manas and the vital force, with the eyes and ears, with earth, water, air and the ether, with fire, and what is other than fire, with desire and the absence of desire, with anger and the absence of anger, with righteousness and unrighteousness, with everything—identified, as is well known, with this (what is perceived) and with that (what is inferred). As it does and acts, so it becomes; by doing good it becomes good, and by doing evil it becomes evil - it becomes virtuous through good acts and vicious through evil acts. Others, however, say, 'The self is identified with desire alone. What it desires, it resolves; what it resolves, it works out; and what it works out, it attains.' (Verse 4.4.5)

Karma is directly related to rebirth. Karma is a basic concept, rebirth is a derivative concept. With origins in ancient India, Rebirth is a fundamental concept of Hinduism, Buddhism, Jainism, Sikhism and Taoism.

Rebirth is a concept that all living beings go through a cycle of multiple births. The rebirth may be in an altogether different situation, realm or form. The situation in which rebirth happens depends upon the seeds of Karma sowed in the past lives. The Soul just transmigrates into another physical Body and starts a new life to reap these seeds. This cycle of birth, death and rebirth continues indefinitely.

Therefore, it is believed that the only things that remain constant are the Soul and the Mind. The Soul keeps getting reincarnated in new physical bodies, torturing one physical Body after another, generating more Karmas and passing their brunt in the future births/ lifetimes/ incarnations.

Let us quickly go through what each religion tells us about Karma.

HINDUISM

Theory of Karma has evolved over centuries in Hinduism.

The earliest Upanishads began with the questions about how and why man is born, and what happens after death. The ancient scholars in Hinduism claimed that those who seek material gains and have materialistic desires, always come back into another life, whereas those who seek spiritual knowledge slowly and steadily climb higher paths of God and finally break the cycle of reincarnation and do not take birth again.

There are many examples of the theory of Karma and its key elements being repeatedly recited in religious text books and folk stories of the Hindu Religion. E.g.

Mahabharta, xii. 291.22

> **"As a man himself sows, so he himself reaps; no man inherits the good or evil act of another man. The fruit is of the same quality as the action".**

SIKHISM

Sikhism also accepts and acknowledges the Hindu belief in Karma and rebirth. The Gurbani accepts Karma as the Law of Nature. Sikhism preaches that we have taken birth because of our Karma. Bad deeds would lead to bad Karma and therefore suffering. Good Deeds would lead to Good Karma.

BUDDHISM

The Law of Karma is a fundamental doctrine in Buddhism. Though the concept of Karma was prevalent in India much before the origination of Buddhism, it was very nicely explained and formulated by Buddha. Buddha explained the reasons behind many facts e.g.

- Why are some people so poor whereas some are so rich?
- Why there exists inequality amongst mankind?
- Why some people are born so intelligent whereas the others so dumb?
- Why some babies have congenital problems e.g. deafness, blindness etc.?
- Why some people are criminals whereas the others are saints?

- How is it that some of us are born with certain traits e.g. some people are naturally born artists, some are naturally good with numbers whereas some are naturally good at debates.

So what exactly is the reason for this inequality or difference that we have in our personality, behaviour or situation? There has to be some cause for it, it can't be accidental. Buddhism, like Hinduism explains this again as a cause and effect phenomenon i.e. it is the result of our own past actions and our own present doings. The Buddha once said—

> **"All living beings have actions (Karma) as their own, their inheritance, their congenital cause, their kinsman, their refuge. It is Karma that differentiates beings into low and high states."**

We definitely inherit hereditary characteristics from our parents, however, the Karmic tendencies accumulated by us over thousands of previous lives play a much larger role in forming our physical and mental characteristics than the ones inherited from our parents.

Is one bound to reap all that one has sown in just proportion?

The Buddha provides an answer :

> **"If anyone says that a man or woman must reap in this life according to his present deeds, in that case there is no religious life, nor is an opportunity afforded for the entire extinction of sorrow. But if anyone says that what a man or woman reaps in this and future lives accords with his or her deeds present and past, in that case there is a religious life, and an opportunity is afforded for the entire extinction of a sorrow." (Anguttara Nikaya)**

When this is the case then why Soul meddles with our life and come with its own life plan?

It is stated in the *Dhammapada* that "not in the sky, nor in mid-ocean, or entering a mountain cave is found that place on earth where one may escape from (the consequences of) an evil deed", yet one is not bound to play all the past arrears of one's Karma. If such were the case emancipation would be impossibility. External recurrence would be the unfortunate result."

Then why do we still live in the current in despair?

JAINISM

Karma is the basic principle within the most important psycho-cosmology in Jainism.

Human moral actions form the basis of the transmigration of the Soul (jīva). The Soul is constrained to a cycle of rebirth, trapped within the material world (saṃsāra), until it finally achieves liberation (mokṣa).

Karma is thought of as a kind of pollution that taints the Soul with various colors (leśyā). Based on its Karma, a Soul undergoes transmigration and reincarnates in various states of existence—like heavens or hells, or as humans or animals. So it troubles Body as it needs it to fulfil its needs.

> **"There is nothing mightier in the world than Karma; Karma tramples down all powers, as an elephant a clump of lotuses."**

The doctrine of Karma is not considered simply in relation to one life-time, but also in relation to both future incarnations and past lives. *Uttarādhyayana-sūtra* 3.3–4 states :

> **"Karma is the root of birth and death. The Souls bound by Karma go round and round in the cycle of existence."**

Unlike Hinduism and Buddhism, in Jainism Karma is considered to be like a subtle matter or particles or a flowing mass of energy which enters a living Body with each activity of the later and envelops it in dark gloom. Karma binds the Soul to the matter and makes its liberation an increasingly difficult task.

When the Soul knows this then why is it playing games of Karmic Cycles?

TAOISM

Karma is an important concept in Taoism. Every deed is tracked by deities and spirits. Appropriate rewards or retribution follow Karma, just like a shadow follows a person.

CHRISTIANITY

Mary Jo Meadow suggests Karma is akin to "Christian notions of sin and its effects."

She states that the Christian teaching on last judgment according to one's charity is a teaching on Karma. Christianity also teaches morals such as reap what one sows (Galatians 6:7) and live by the sword, die by the sword (Matthew 26:52).

Having gone through the above excerpts, the question arises—

What is the point of reincarnating?

Why do I have to take so many births?

Let us take an example here – Every day, when I wake up, my objective is to go to my workplace and work upon various tasks. These may include – complete the tasks which have been pending for a long time, start working upon new tasks, progress on tasks which have been going on, assign tasks to my team members, and do status reporting on tasks to my peers and/or seniors. Now, to go to office, I may decide to drive my car, or may be take a bus or a tram or any other means of transport. The overall objective of why I am doing this is to move ahead or grow in my career, for my betterment, to succeed in life, to reach a point in life where I can feel satisfied.

We can also compare this concept with how in a company daily accounts are planned and managed with the ultimate aim to make the company touch the highest success graph. To achieve this—

- A Daily tracker of income and expense is maintained
- Payment reminders are sent and Budgeting is done
- Control on expenses is exercised to increase savings

Similarly, think of our Body as the vehicle for our Soul. So, before the Soul takes birth, it make a list of Karmas which we need to work upon and settle down in the forthcoming birth.

These are the Karmas which I would have created with various people in my past incarnations. The point to be noted here is that we have created so many Karmas over so many incarnations with so many people, that we can't settle all of them in one single incarnation. So, similar to our daily task list, in which we enlist the tasks we would work upon on a single day, we prepare a Karma plan wherein we enlist the Karmas we would settle, with selected people in the forthcoming incarnation.

Now the question is—

Is there a need for all this drama?

Is it not making my life difficult and torturing my Body?

The Karmic cycle in many cases is taking me in past instead of future progress. This can continue in an endless loop. What we mean is that in this life, the victim became the culprit, in next life; the culprit can become the victim and so on and so forth. So you see how the Soul plays such dirty games with one's Body.

Also, it is true that we reincarnate in Karmic relationships i.e. with the same people but in different constellations. A person, who is your husband, could have been your brother/sister, mother/father or anyone else in any or more of your past lives. So, if you find yourself in a difficult marriage or relationship, but you are still not able to leave each other, mostly it is a Karmic relationship and either you or your partner must have wronged the other one and that is some Karmic lessons you both have to learn from or with each other.

When a past life ended badly, the law of cause and effect will follow you in all your next lives, until the issue is resolved. Now the question arises, consciously we do not remember any of our past lives or our past Karmas. We do not even remember the faces or names of people with whom we have created these Karmas. Neither do we have any memories of our past lives. Is this all not torturous for us?

You may say that we are actually victims of the Soul, because consciously we do not remember any of our past life actions and therefore, we are not even aware of why we are being tortured, humiliated, insulted or victimized. It would of some help if we could remember what we did in our past life to deserve this in the current life time.

A more desirable situation would be, where all was sorted out in that very life time and there was no need to carry forward and bear the trauma of that life. Why should I bear the burnt when some other Body was involved in the crime? It is all the doing of the Soul. He is happily watching this game, playing with our sentiments, emotions and giving physical troubles in the form of diseases, disappointments, fears, phobias, heartbreaks etc.

Have you ever wondered from where all these are coming? Who is providing all the data? The culprit here is that part of the Mind which has stored all the details of past lives and thus provides the desired data to help the Soul in making or drafting its next life plan. So it is not wrong to say that along with Soul, Mind is equally guilty and partner in crime.

Chapter Three

The Mind : Our Balance Sheet

Our Mind is like a huge database or balance sheet that the Soul maintains. It has billions of entries of debit and credits in the account book of life. The Soul ensures that all that we do in life, whether good or bad is all recorded in the Mind, so that it can use this information later on to play with our Body. Let us analyse this throuth same example—

1. *"Few months ago, I went to a birthday party, where I had a chocolate cake, its taste was very different. Since then, I have been to many birthday parties and have had chocolate cakes; however none had the same taste. How is it possible that I still remember that unique taste?"*
2. *"About 3 years ago, I went for an important seminar, where I got into a heated argument with a stranger. Today, I accidently bumped into this person at a shopping mall. As soon as I saw him, I could recall each and every sentence he had said to me 3 years back and that gave me goose bumps because I thought I have forgotten that incidence. From where is this information coming from?"*

3. *"At the age of 8, I got stuck in the lift; it gives me chills down my spine if I remember that incident even now. I am 40 now, why am I still scared of using the lifts and why does it gives me the same uncomfortable feeling whenever I enter any lift?"*
4. *"At a wedding, I met a person, whom I have never met in life, however, I got this strange feeling that I have known her forever and I think she also felt the same! From where does this information coming from?"*
5. *"Since birth I am very scared of rivers; to an extent that even if I go near a swimming pool, I start getting anxious and start shivering and perspiring. This is creating an unwanted phobia and keeping me away from going near any type of water body. I cannot even think of going for a beach holiday, or a cruise for that matter. I have no bad experience to link with, so from where is this fear coming from?"*

Most of us can relate to or rather have already gone through similar situations at some point in our lives and mostly we have no logical explanation to them. As we go through this chapter we will be able to find some of the answers.

We have already talked in details about the Soul and the Karma in the previous Chapters. So let us talk about what is The Mind. Since the Soul is part of the main consciousness, also called as Creator, it considers itself equal to the Supreme Power and thus shows arrogance and high- headedness. It has started to manipulate the Mind, which is another form of metaphysical energy to provide data to the Consciousness.

WHAT IS MIND?

In a layman's term, Brain and Mind are one or one and the same thing. A lot of times, people use the terms brain and Mind interchangeably, which is not true. Mind is an energy form whereas Brain is a physical part/ organ of our Body which also becomes dead along the Body when Soul leaves the Body. Upon Death, the Mind leaves the Body, to go along with the Soul.

Some clairvoyant people have described Mind as a big ball of Energy around every physical Body which stretches up to 12 feet in diameter. This ball of Energy is equal in size for every person, be it a child or an adult.

The Soul continuously sends message units to the Mind as per its own needs. Based on these message units, received from the Soul, the Mind sends electrical impulses to the brain which in turn sends signals through a well-defined nervous system to various parts of the Body, to function in a particular manner.

For its convenience, the Soul has made two different compartments in the Mind—

Conscious Mind : The data of day to day activity. You may consider it is as our Current account.

Subconscious Mind : The records of current life Memories and all the previous lives that we have already lived. The subconscious mind is the Saving account and Fixed deposit. It is this part mainly where the Soul draws and maintains the Balance sheet.

Now we can easily define what the Mind is and what role its each division plays. Let us also see, which part of the Mind plays the dirtiest role.

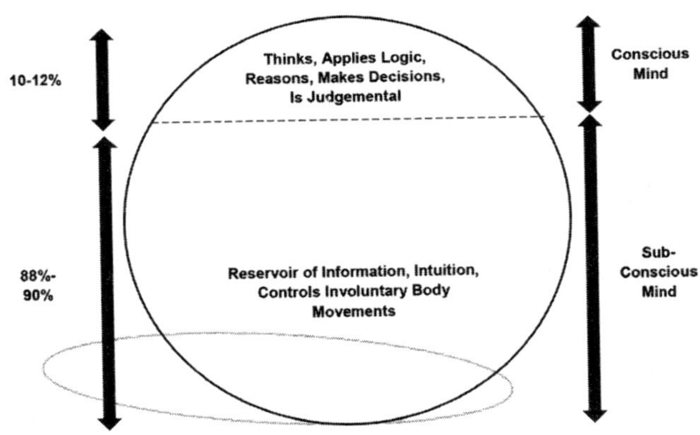

WHAT IS CONSCIOUS MIND?

Conscious Mind, which forms only 10-12% of our total Mind, is that portion of the Mind which is analytical, judgmental and takes decisions, based on the inputs received on day to day basis.

The question arises from where do we receive input from? We can receive inputs from different sources such as our environment- newspapers, television, other people, circumstances, hot, cold, sound, smell, taste, touch, pressure etc., and also from our own Body parts e.g. pain in some part of the Body, tanning of skin, allergy, hunger, thirst, comfort, etc.

Based on all these inputs, we take every day decisions. To understand how, let us first understand what the sub-conscious Mind is all about.

WHAT IS SUB-CONSCIOUS MIND?

Consciously we do not record our present life events nor remember any of our past lives or our past Karmas. We do not even remember the faces or names of people with whom we created these Karmas. We do not have any memories of our past lives. So where do all these memories reside? These memories are directly emerging from the Sub-conscious Mind.

Sub-conscious Mind forms about 88-90% of our total Mind. It is like a big reservoir of information.

Sub-conscious mind further has two divisions—

1. *One, which has the records of all the events from our current life is like a saving account or Fixed Deposit.*
2. *One which has the records of all the events from our past lives i.e. all our karmic investments, assets or liabilities are registered here.*

Therefore, the sub-conscious Mind is rightly said to be the reservoir of information and it stores all memories and experiences from Current Life and all our Past Lives. All significant events from all our current life and past lives and all memories – good, bad, loving, traumatic, hurtful, painful etc. are all stored in the sub-conscious Mind.

Even our ability of being intuitive comes from the sub-conscious Mind. This intuition again may be coming from our current life memory or from our past life memories in the current scenario.

This 'intuition' may be creating a feeling of unrest, sadness, dissatisfaction, phobia, fear, physical problem, relationship issue or discomfort in the physical Body. Migraine, diabetes, cancer, Arthritis are been passed on from generation to generation as per our medical science. It will be correct to say that they are right because according to us they are being passed on to us from life after life. The curses and vows (which are the bad debts in life's balance sheet) already as per our Indian scriptures are being passed on from generation to generation and both the families and the individual bodies suffer because of them.

You may say, that we meet so many people every day, but we don't remember everyone or everything that happened with us on daily basics. Yes, you are right, only significant incidents and people (which are our Assets or Liabilities in life's balance sheet) get stored in our sub-conscious Mind.

In the beginning of this chapter we talked about the bitter experience of a person with a total stranger three years back and how he could recall it back when he happened to bump into him once again.

When we asked the person what was so special about that particular cake? His answer was-"I remembered the taste of that particular chocolate cake as it was very unique and I really liked it. I do not however remember the taste of all other cakes I have had since my childhood!"

The trauma of being stuck in the lift at the age of 8, still troubles him even as a grown-up person.

All the above incidences are related to the current life memories and are coming from the Modern memory section of the Subconscious Mind.

So, every event which touches us emotionally or physically, leaves an impact upon us, and gets stored in our sub-conscious mind. This is how we could remember all these people and incidents from 1 to 3. Whereas incidences listed from 4th point onwards are coming from the Past life Memory section of Subconscious Mind, where records of all our Past life memories are stored.

Talking about point number 4, the lady might have looked familiar, because she might have met her in one of her past lives and that information is stored in her sub-conscious Mind. Sometimes, you may feel much attached to a person for no special reason.

Similarly, you may dislike a few people for no obvious reason. You may even get a feeling of hatred towards a person for no specific reason. If you do, then trust us, it is some Karma from one of your past lives which is making you behave or feel like this.

Again, in example number 5, this fear of water is actually not a fear, but a phobia because it has been there since the birth. All phobias come from past lives. The person may have drowned to death in one of his past lives, or may be someone really close to him might have drowned in water in front of him. The fear, pain and emotional trauma were so great that the event and the fear of water got stored in his sub-conscious Mind.

We have talked about diseases passing on from one generation to another, even when a person has a very healthy lifestyle in the current life and he is very spiritual, God fearing and compassionate. This is nothing but our liabilities in the life's balance sheet and yet another game of Soul- seeking pleasure by hurting the Body.

Even bad habits like substance abuse in a person may also be coming from the past life. Ask a person who is addicted to say smoking about how he felt the first time he smoked. He may tell you that his first experience was terrible and he really didn't like it, still continued for some reason. Someone else may tell you that it felt familiar and he could easily smoke. This case is a past life case of addiction to smoking. The sub-conscious Mind is so well attuned to the feeling of smoking that the person very easily picks up the habit of smoking.

The question is – when the Soul has already experienced it in that life time, what is the need to have this memory from a past life which is creating a concern in one's current life, Again the same 'thought'–what is the need to remember that is long gone by? Is this not the dirty game the Soul is playing with us just because it wants to come back again and again and enjoy, laugh, feel happy and satisfied when it sees that the Body has to face the brunt of the atrocities created by the Soul's selfish games of Reincarnation?

The Soul has purposely made the Sub-Conscious Mind much larger and stronger than our physical Body. The sub-conscious Mind is taking charge of our life at the behest of

Soul and we are made to merely enact or to play like puppets. We are sure none of us would like that to happen and all of us wants to consider our Body's happiness first.

To take charge of our life back we have to try our best to control the Sub-conscious Mind, otherwise the opposite will keep on happening. Happiness of our Body is basically our happiness and that is what we all are striving for.

So from above we can summarize that the Soul has collected all the data because it needed so from our Past Life happenings and based on it decides or works upon the current life plan and puts us into a never ending viscous cycle of Karma.

Chapter Four

The Body : Our Current Asset

Life as created by the Creator is a combination of 3 things- the Body, the Mind and the Soul. Previously we have discussed about the Soul and the Mind, let us understand about our Body. Our body can be understood better as our current Asset, as the Soul attains a new Body in every incarnation, depending upon the balance sheet of Karmas, that the Soul has created in our Mind. It even changes the shape and color of the Body, it brings in differences in the physical appearances of bodies, thereby creating more troubles and differences among human beings, a sense of comparison and competition.

For the Body every living being is the same and it does not differentiate between the size, shape, colour or creed. These differences are being understood by the 'conscious mind' which is always judgmental. It is this which brings about the differentiation at the behest of the Soul which actually is playing this dirty game of creating rifts among Humans.

Who are you? said the Caterpillar.

This was not an encouraging opening for a conversation.

Alice replied, rather shyly, "I...I hardly know, Sir, just at present—at least I know who I was when I got up this morning, but I think I must have been changed several times since then..."

Alice's Adventures in Wonderland, by Lewis Carroll

This is the beautiful reality of being in a Human form! From just a single cell, to a fetus, then to a baby, and then progressing a child –to a grownup person and ending life post old age, we are always growing, always changing. Our Body is working round the clock, 7 days a week and 365 days in a year. Our Body is helping us to experience various mysteries of life.

Human Body is considered to be the most evolved creation of the universe, and is studied in utmost details by various paradigms, each giving their own interpretations to what is it all about and what it is made of, but so far a complete revelation of its mysteries has not happened.

The Science rightly says that our Body is a big super smart Chemical factory. Our Body has independent departments such as nervous system, digestive system, respiratory system, circulatory system, reproductive system, lymphatic system etc., which works independently and in perfect harmony with each other and with different organs and body parts.

The human Body is also often described as a large vessel containing chemicals that are constantly reacting with each other and thus bringing changes, development and growth. Almost 99% of the mass of the human Body is made up of six chemicals or elements: oxygen, carbon, hydrogen, nitrogen, calcium, and phosphorus and about 0.85% is composed of another five elements: potassium, sulfur, sodium, chlorine, and magnesium. All these 11 elements are necessary for life.

According to Science our Body composition is made of 70 percent of water and rest of the Body mass comes from fats, proteins and minerals. Our Body is an amalgam of physical, mechanical, chemical and electrodynamic energies.

Our Body can also experience through the senses of touch, hearing, smell, visual and taste by the use of Body organs. There are five sensory organs present in our Body. They are eyes, nose, ears, tongue, and skin. Skin is the largest sensory organs in our body as it covers the whole body. Nose is used for smelling, Eye is used for vision, Ear is used for hearing (audios). Tongue is used for finding different types of tastes.

The five sense helps us to deal with the world around us. The role of these five senses is to receive the information from the world, after which the information is carried to the brain, than the brain passes the response and then these senses respond accordingly.

In Hindu literature, five senses are described as the "five material faculties" (pañcannaṃ indriyānaṃ avakanti). They appear in allegorical representation as early as in the Katha Upanishad (roughly 6th century BC), as five horses drawing the "chariot" of the Body, guided by the Mind as "chariot driver" and Soul the "Master".

According to Ayurveda, the Body is made of five elements (tattwas). All yoga practices, yoga therapies, traditional Indian Medicines work on these five elements- The Earth, Fire, Water, Air and Ether/Space. Knowledge of the five elements allows the yogi to understand the laws of nature and to use yoga to attain greater health, power, knowledge, wisdom and happiness.

Each of these five elements represents a state of matter. Earth is not just soil, but it is everything in nature that is solid.

Water is everything that is liquid. Air is everything that is in gaseous form. Fire is that part of Nature that transforms one state of matter into another. For example, fire transforms the solid state of water (ice) into liquid water and then into its gaseous state (steam). Withdrawing fire recreates the solid state. Ether or Space is the mother of the other elements. The experience of space as luminous emptiness is the basis of higher spiritual experiences.

Each element is responsible for different structures in the Body. Earth forms solid structures, such as bones, flesh, skin, tissues, and hair. Water forms saliva, urine, semen, blood, and sweat. Fire forms hunger, thirst, and sleep. Air is responsible for all movement, including expansion, contraction, and suppression. Space forms physical attraction and repulsion, as well as fear. Earth and water are at the base, below the navel, fire is in the middle of the torso; air and space reside in the upper Body.

The magnificence of our Body can be best understood with the knowledge that it is not just a physical structure but it has a complete energy system associated with it. The Body is strong, powerful and conducts activities for the enrichment of the Soul & the Mind. Unfortunately, the position of the Body has been reduced to be that of a helpless slave by the Soul and the Mind. The Body is totally in their control, when it should be the opposite.

THE HUMAN ENERGY SYSTEM, THE AURA, SUBTLE BODIES & CHAKRAS

By now we are all quite familiar with our physical bodies and their functions, now let's try to understand our Body's subtle energy systems which is actually created from and sustained by the energetic layers that are outside of our normal vision.

These energetic layers or subtle bodies create an interconnected field of energy around the physical Body that is commonly known as the auric field. Each subtle Body connects into the physical Body via an energy point or chakra, which directs the energy into the physical Body via the meridian system. In alternative medicine, an "aura" refers to an electromagnetic energy field which encapsulates a human Body, an animal, a plant or any non-living object. We believe that any living or non-living thing has an energy field, or a subtle Body which is called an Aura around it.

The Aura consists of seven layers or auric energy, also known as the physical, astral, lower, higher, cellular, intuitional, and absolute planes. Each of these energies has its own unique frequency. They are interrelated, and each etheric energy affects the others. They also affect a person's feelings, emotions, thought patterns, behaviour, and overall health. A state of imbalance in one of the energy field leads to a state of imbalance in the others. Although they cannot be seen by the naked eyes, they can be seen psychically through the third eye or with the aid of Kirlian camera / Aura photography.

The term subtle body describes the various layers of vibrating energy that make up a human being beyond the obvious physical layer. As you move outwards from the physical Body into the auric field, each subtle energy vibrates at a slightly faster vibration than the one before it. So the etheric energy is faster than the physical and the emotional energy is faster than the etheric energy etc. Each of these different layers of energy, including the one we recognize as the physical Body interpenetrates the others to work as a complete system.

We as humans are always and constantly under self-questioning :

- Who are 'We'?
- Why are 'We' here?
- What is the purpose of the Creator of sending us here on Earth?

WHO ARE 'WE'?

According to the Bible, Adam and Eve were the first man and woman created from the dust by God and sent on Earth to the Sacred Garden to live happily ever after. From the Garden they were permitted to eat fruits of all the trees except one, the tree of the knowledge of good and evil, Eve was tempted by a talking serpent to eat the forbidden fruit, and gives some to Adam, who eats too. God curses all three, the man to a lifetime of hard labor followed by death, the woman to the pain of childbirth and to subordination to her husband, and the serpent to go on his belly and suffer the enmity of both man and woman. God then clothed the nakedness of the man and woman, who have become god-like in knowing good and evil, then banished them from the garden lest they eat the fruit of a second tree, the tree of life, and find the knowledge to live forever. So the God also created Death on achieving which the mankind will return back to dust, to the very source of its origin.

Point to ponder upon—Who is this Serpent? What was its intention in tempting Eve to eat the forbidden fruit from the forbidden tree and in the process, not only change the pattern of their life but also the life of their progeny forever? Isn't this the selfish plan of the Soul, who wants to experience through the Body-both good and bad, Pleasure and pain, riches and poverty, health and sickness and in the process makes the Body suffer. Is this all a part of the Soul's Plan at the macro level?

WHY ARE WE HERE?

It is a question that can best be answered by looking again at how the Bible explains it. Genesis Chapter 1, once God completed creating the heavens and the earth, the plant life and all the animals, he created mankind and spoke well of the male and female and showed his pleasure by entrusting them with his creation :

> **"So God created man in His own image, in the image of God created He him; male and female created He them and God blessed them, and God said unto them, be fruitful, and multiply, and replenish the earth"**

WHAT IS OUR PURPOSE?

Osho has very rightly explained this—

> **"Each person comes into this world with a specific destiny- he has something to fulfill, some message has to be delivered, and some work has to be completed. You are not here accidentally, you are here meaningfully. There is a purpose behind you. The whole intend is to do something through you."**

There is a reason that we are all here in this world, and it is all about the discovering of our own Self. It is only when we are aware of that who we are, that we can go on and discover what we can bring. We are just brilliant! We are a creation of the 'Infinite' here on earth. And we have brought our own self here through a process of creation.

The trouble started when our main consciousness which is our Soul became arrogant and started manipulating our Mind. Mind which then affected our conscious mind and finally our own thought process became maligned and started comparing our own body with others. We started seeing our own self as the image that we see in the mirror. Even that is a warped image, as our Mind is telling us that we are too big, too dark, too tall, not pretty enough, not rich enough etc. and Mind did not stop here, it started to see these follies on every other Body.

This becomes our reality and stored in the form of ego which brings a sense of competition and is the root cause of our anxiety.

Here is where our Mind started playing tricks on us on behest of Soul. Since the Soul started to manipulate the Mind, for the Soul, Mind was nothing but just an energy form to provide data. So the drama started and in due course our Body got involved in it inadvertently, and from here all the problems started for the Body.

NOW LET'S SEE WHAT THE 'BODY' FEELS ABOUT THE WHOLE SITUATION

> **"My (Body) whole purpose of life shifted to just act as a slave to the Soul and Mind. They are making use of me as just a body to get their work done as per their plan, and whims & fancies. I am just a rented house for the Soul and Mind. They rent out a new Body every time they come up with a new plan to come back to this planet Earth."**

> **"The Soul uses my each and every cell and tissues, to fulfill its desires to experience good versus bad, various positive and negative emotions, simple and traumatic life. For this purpose it makes me go through these transformations-conception, birth, growth, sustenance, reproduction, degradation and finally death. At the time of death the Soul abandons me (the Body) and leave it lifeless like a piece of dead wood."**

"For the Soul I am just an integrated piece of flesh with various organs, muscles, ducts, cells, bones etc. ,which are further made of material elements-solids, liquids, gases, etc. and exist for a limited period of time. 'I' the 'Body' is born, grows to maturity, produces offspring, and then gradually deteriorate, and stops functioning when the Soul leaves me and then I go back into the dust. My purpose of existence is to provide shelter and to work like a machine for the Soul and Mind. I have no identity as I am different in each Body form. The name given to me is also not mine alone, as you can find many Bodies with the same name."

"When I am alive I am loved, respected and called by my name, but immediately after Death (when the Soul leaves me), I am called a Body. So there goes, my identity for a toss again."

So in a nutshell, one can say, the Body is like a helpless puppet in the hands of the Soul who is manipulating and torturing it—

- By using the balance sheet of Karma created in the Mind
- By creating Soul Plan i.e. life and death.
- Through Soul fragments and attachments.
- By further developing Fears and Phobias.

Let us discuss one by one what effect these have on the Body and understand whether they were actually needed or not.

Chapter Five

The Soul's Business Plan

ANIMOSITY BETWEEN MOTHER AND SON

This was a very unique case. In our Indian culture, mother and son share a very special bond of care and affection. A man in his late sixties came to us with a very unusual issue he was not able to forgive his own mother who was not even alive and the emotion of hatred was slowly killing him from inside. The reason for this hatred was that the mother made many unsuccessful attempts to kill him during his childhood.

Even today he looks back in horror at his childhood days where many times he was very brutally beaten and was almost left to die by the mother. They shared mutual hatred for each other. When he was just 6 years old his father shifted him to his paternal grandparents to save his life from his own mother.

In the Post Life Regression (PLR) session this person went into a lifetime where he was a snake happily living in a burrow surrounded by rocks in a field with its partner. The partner had recently laid eggs. They both were eagerly waiting for the eggs to hatch and to see their young ones.

In the close proximity a young farmer (the current life mother) was ploughing the field, totally ignorant about the existence of the snake family. While ploughing the field his axe hit the snake's burrow and damaged the eggs. Now the snake become very furious and in a fit of rage, it bits the farmer. The farmer also makes an attempt to kill the snake but then snake manages to wriggle out and escape.

The dying farmer who was the sole earning member of his family which included small children and ailing parents, turned very furious and worried and takes the oath of teaching the snake a lesson someday.

To teach the snake a lesson and also to take his revenge, this farmer planned to come back as his mother in this current lifetime and made all the efforts to kill her son, but just like previous life, he had been escaping from all her attempts and surviving.

A GRIEVING HUSBAND OVER WIFE'S DEATH

There was a gentleman who had come over in a very depressed state of Mind. His wife had recently passed away after suffering from cancer for over 5 years. Being at a very good position in a large organization, this gentleman had not left even one stone unturned to save his wife. He got the best treatments done from the best doctors in the best hospitals of India. Not only this, he had himself taken care of his wife every second, trying to provide all the emotional and physical support he could have. However, one fine day, his wife was put on a ventilator and finally she passed away. He was deeply hurt because he loved his wife too much.

With all the moments he had spent during these last 5 years with his wife, trying to research on all the best cancer treatments etc., he felt guilty that he could not save his beloved wife. He was under a lot of emotional trauma and was suffering from excessive guilt.

During his session, he was able to talk to the Soul of his wife. She told him that her cancer was part of the Soul Plan. It was necessary because his Soul had to learn a lesson of caring, loving, giving, being responsible and patient. She also mentioned to him that she knows that he had done everything that was possible on earth to save her life and that he should not feel guilty at all. It was all planned in their mutually agreed Soul Plan, which they created for themselves before taking birth.

THE SOUL PLAN

So, do you now understand that any of our sufferings or pleasures in our current life is because of the seeds of Karma, that the Soul made us sow in our past lives or is making us sow in the current life too? Does the Soul want us to be always caught up in this vicious cycle of Karma and never live peacefully?

Have you ever wondered, who actually decides what our life would be like based on our Karmas? Who plans for our next life?

You will be surprised to know that it is our own Soul which makes a complete outline of our life plan for the upcoming incarnation. This plan is called the the Soul Plan. The Soul goes through vigorous planning both at Macro and Micro levels.

This is like making a project report for setting up a new project where we decide what to do. In this we first decide our purpose, then how to achieve it. What resources will be available and to be gathered. How to implement the project and what results to be expected. Now in order to have a successful project we look for the most suitable location where the project is to be installed and the participants who will take the best care.

WHAT IS THE MACRO LEVEL PLAN?

The macro level or the broad level plan of the Soul is prepared based on mainly the Karmic balances it needs to settle down and lessons it needs to learn in the forthcoming incarnation.

So for this, it decides the main purpose of its next incarnation and depending upon the purpose of its next life, it chalks out the detailed macro level plan.

While doing so, the most important and most crucial part is to come up with an ideal environment where it will take birth. It should be the environment which will enable the Soul to fulfil its Karmic goals and its life purpose.

The Macro level planning mainly includes the following—

1. *The kind of parents, siblings and relatives—the basic nature of the parents, siblings or close relatives and the number of family members.*
2. *The family environment e.g. orthodox, conservative, broad-Minded, cohesive, supportive, indifferent, conflictual, loving, distressed, physically abusive, emotionally abusive, impoverished, single-parent, father-headed, mother-headed, functional, dysfunctional.*
3. *The family's social standing – It means what is the status or social class or the position of the family in the society. It can also refer to how well the family is viewed by the society based on the caste (for caste based systems) or the educational status of the family members or the achievements of the family members in various fields like art, sports or education etc., or the inherited status of the family.*

- The family's financial standing–This refers to how well are the finances of the family e.g., rich, poor or middle class or any intermediate level between the main 3 levels.
- The circumstances or situations in which I would take birth.
- The place and family I would take birth in.
- Would I take birth as a male or a female or a transgender?
- Would I take birth with any physical disabilities e.g. deafness, blindness etc.
- Would I take birth with any mental disabilities?
- What challenges would I meet at different points in my life?
- What physical or emotional traumas would I suffer from?
- The diseases I would suffer from at different points in life.
- What all Karmas from my past incarnations I would settle in this incarnation?
- To do so, what all people would be a part of my life or which people I would meet at different points in my life?
- What career would I choose?
- What would be the significant events of my life?
- How would I die? Would it be a natural death or an accidental death or death from sickness or a torturous death?

And the list goes on...

Basically, the Soul has to plan according to the purpose it wants to fulfill and the lessons it wants to learn in the upcoming life. In every birth, the Soul needs to settle certain Karmas from one or more past lives. Therefore a very detailed planning is done by the Soul in terms of selecting the lives whose Karmic baggage needs to be settled, then selecting the Soul group with which it would reincarnate, the circumstances etc. and also its next life's purpose.

1. *The purpose of the Soul of physically or mentally disabled children may be to make their parents learn a lesson of patience and to strengthen their relationship.*
2. *Two enemies may decide to take birth as siblings to sort out their enmity.*
3. *A Soul which has just spent a life as a very rich person, may decide to take birth as a beggar to experience poverty.*
4. *A wife who was tortured by her husband may decide to take birth in the same family to seek revenge.*
5. *A male who may have raped a few females in his lifetime, may decide to take birth as a female with a life plan in which to get raped to learn and experience how emotionally and physically painful it is.*
6. *A wife betrayed by her husband may take birth with a life plan to betray her husband in her next incarnation.*

Overall, the Soul indulges in a lot of selfish planning before it take its next birth. Each life is like a year's account book. Where all the accounts of different lives of good and bad deeds are written back in the Mind. Each year has assets and liabilities, profit and loss, debtors and creditors which basically are the experiences of life after life.

Based on the data collected during the last life journey and the previous lives, the Soul consults its Balance Sheet in the Mind energy and then plans for the next Birth/ Incarnation.

This projected Balance Sheet is then utilized to observe where and how to meet these people/Souls whose assets & liabilities are to be squared with. In which family there is a possibility of the childbirth and to achieve the maximum from the plan. The child/ the Body does not have the right to choose the parents. It is the Soul who has this privilege.

So, once everything has been chalked out, the Soul waits for the fertilization of the egg of it's would be mother. Fertilization happens and then the baby grows very rapidly inside the mother's womb and finally, when the Soul decides, the birth of this baby takes place.

Soul finally takes another reincarnation with the set of new Life Plan–the New Business Plan.

Souls always take birth in groups or choose the same set of Souls in different relationships in each incarnations with whom they have to settle some scores.

This is because the Soul makes us create Karmas with people we spend the most time with and for the purpose of settlement of those Karmas, the best suited scenario will be to take birth in close proximity.

DNA OF A BABY

We all know the definition of the DNA according to medical science, which is DNA is the hereditary material in humans and it is present in nearly all cells of a human Body. It encodes the genetic instructions used in the development and functioning of all known living organisms.

To add another angle to this definition, the DNA contains information carried forward from the father's DNA, the mother's DNA and now besides this, another set of DNA is that of the Soul, which is called the Spiritual DNA, the DNA of what the Soul has planned.

Now you may ask what kind of information does the spiritual DNA carry? The spiritual DNA carries the information which is present in the Macro level plan created by the Soul for the upcoming birth. This combination of the two that of the child and the Spiritual DNA may match (in most of the cases) but there are chances of a mismatch and thus leads to further complications. This is yet another way of the Soul to torture the Body.

Why should Soul interfere in this too? This gives rise to another concept–the Micro Plan.

MICRO PLAN

In any industry or company we develop some minor changes based on the environment and surroundings. Thus have to bring about a change in our debtors and creditors to adjust and square off. Why cannot our government make it mandatory to set off debtors and creditors in the same year? This will also make my Body to adjust to this concept and clear everything in the Current life.

Since, the Micro plan comes in the hands of the human Body to control & support. How well the Human Body is able to understand and take action is what matters to make life smooth, peaceful and progressive. To play this role well, the Body is dependent upon many, more factors. We may enumerate them as the—

- environment and surroundings
- family culture and upbringing
- partners, spouse, relatives, peers, friends
- locational changes

- job profiles
- financial progress
- and such many mores

All these have an impact on Body's behavior, attitude, thinking, working, progress, reactions and thus it brings about a change in Soul's Plan.

For example: Going back to what the Soul had planned, say if some untoward event or happening takes place in my family or with parents and they lose all money, may not thus be able to provide me with that sort of education my Soul had planned, I may not get that support, thus have to struggle for what I was destined for, my scenario changes. There may be a possibility that instead of becoming a Doctor, I may land up to be a compounder or even in some other line of activities.

Now based on this new line of activity, and to survive the circumstances, it brings about a change in the Soul's plan which will be at the Micro level changes, as it will be dependent on the day to day basis of surroundings, availability & circumstances.

Here the Micro Life plan is totally Conscious Mind based. It is my Conscious Mind, which is judgmental and takes decisions for the betterment, comfort and peace of the Body. There is always a tug of war between the Conscious Mind versus Subconscious Mind.

Imagine a scenario where the Soul has planned to take birth as a female and selected its set of parents, time and place of conception. However during fertilization, the chromosomes from the sperm combine with the chromosomes of the egg in such a manner that instead of a female, a male baby is conceived.

Now the Soul has no other option but to get attached to a male fetus inside the womb. So, the Soul decides to carry on with the conception. Finally, it takes birth in the body of a boy, however, all traits are of a female, e.g. the boy likes to dress up as a female, he has more interest in female games, and he gets attracted towards boys rather than girls.

So, taking birth as a Gay or a Lesbian is the decision the Soul makes at the time of fertilization.

The Soul, as given in the above scenario had planned to take birth as a female, however, the fertilization happened in a way that instead of a female, a male baby is conceived.

The Soul still has a choice to not attach to the baby (as it had planned for a different life purpose) and leave the womb,however it many cases, it attaches itself to the baby. This choice, sometimes, may lead to confusion. That is why you may have heard some people saying—"I am a female trapped in a male body" and vice-versa.

Thus, we see that there is a possibility of flaws in the Soul Plan. This is the point of conflict between the Macro and Micro. It then depends how well my Body is able to accept the changes, what are my circumstances, my surroundings, my conditions of living, and my support system. My tug of war is between what my Soul wants and what my Body wants. Each one has to work for a change. This change creates a lot of new karmic accounts. Many things meant to be completed in this Life are again left undone and many new things are added. So you see this is how life is planned and how the Game Of life is played by the Soul.

Chapter Six

Death
Book Closure of a Year's Account Book

Death equates to closing the year's account book and then updating the records in the Mind with all debits, credits, fixed deposits, assets and liability information. Upon Death, who has to suffer? The Body!

Another important part of the Soul Plan is Death, or more rightly said, "Leaving the Human Body"- this is another dirty Game where the Souls play with Body. The Soul is very selfish, it actually never dies, it just dumps the Body when all its motives which it had planned to do through the Body in a particular lifetime are accomplished. So once the Soul has learnt the lessons and achieved the goals, it leaves the Body.

All the mythologies say that 'who takes birth has to end that life'. The end of life is called Death. Death, when it will come is not known and is controlled mainly by the Soul and sometimes by unforeseen reasons like accident, surgery, war, riots, natural calamities, epidemics etc.

SO HOW DOES DEATH REALLY HAPPEN?

The death happens when the Soul just leaves or detaches itself from the physical Body, which it had adopted as a carrier for its journey as a human. This happens when it has learnt the lessons and achieved the goals which it had planned for in the Soul plan. The Mind Energy stops sending the electrical impulses to the brain which in turn stops the voluntary and involuntary activities of the Body, and then the person is considered to be fully dead.

An average birth to death journey starts when the conception takes place, the Soul along with Mind attaches itself to this Body and gives all its energy and continues to do so for the next twenty five years, that is why the Body grow very rapidly from the stage when fertilization of the Ovum takes place up to first 25 years. From age 25 to 50 there is no further growth in the Body and it remains in same condition as the Soul has stopped giving further energy now. From age 50 to 75 years, the Soul starts taking back its energies which it needs to go back to the Creator. This leads to aging and rapid deterioration of the Body. And this continues till the Soul has taken back all its energy and is now fully prepared for leaving the Body and then a natural Death happens!

WHAT HAPPENS TO THE BODY AFTER DEATH?

We all are aware of all the hardship the Body has to bear when it is alive, unfortunately, its misery does not stop even upon death. Immediately after the death, the Body goes through rapid deterioration, the heart stops beating, there is drastic dropping of body temperature, stiffening or rigor Mortis sets in, decomposition of body tissues, emission of sulphurous gasses with horrific odor, bloating of the body, falling of the tissues, hair and nails, the body swells until it burst open, leaving nothing but the skeleton behind. Due to this reason we dispose of the bodies of our dead ones at the earliest.

Before we proceed further, we would like to mention one more disheartening fact here. Have you ever noticed or observed that when a person is alive, and we talk about that person to someone else, we also refer to them by their name. e.g. "John is sleeping", "Sid went to the shopping mall". However, when the same person dies, we instead say "John's Body is still in the hospital" OR "They have buried Sid's Body in the old cemetery". Would we ever say "John is still in the hospital" to refer to his dead Body? The answer is No.

The reason is that sub-consciously, we all know that Soul and Body are two different things. As long as the Soul is with Body, we use a name to refer to it. However, as soon as the Soul leaves the Body and life ends, it becomes just a dead –decaying Body and all its near and dear ones are in hurry to dispose of this Body and that too very brutally- by burning or burying in deep- dark pit. A Body they loved and cared about, when the Soul was residing in it gets such a horrible treatment once the Soul leaves it. So for Body death is a very traumatic experience.

WHAT HAPPENS TO THE SOUL AFTER DEATH?

In case of the Soul, Death is a happy moment, because death brings it closer to the Creator. It is a point to rejoice for the Soul because he is being relieved from the entrapment inside the Body and will be free now.

Soul reincarnates into a Body to learn and experience through the Body, to gain experiences, to grow spiritually and ultimately become one with the Creator. When the Soul is leaving the body, it is not bothered about the loved ones of the

Body's family members, physical pain the Body has to endure. The Soul just moves out of the Body in eagerness to meet the creator.

There have been other cases in which, in spite of being completely dead i.e. the voluntary as well as the involuntary functions not working, a person has revived in a few seconds or a few minutes time. Such cases occur when the Soul suddenly realizes that it has some unfinished task and it doesn't want to leave now. As we discuss this, it will be worth knowing that once the Soul leaves the Body, it is still present in this dimension for the next 72 hours before moving to a higher dimension.

Therefore, after leaving the human Body, it still has some time before it can finally move on. During this time, the muscles of the human Body still have energy and the blood is intact, therefore the Soul can still come back. However, once the chemical reaction starts in the Body and the organs steadily stops working, then the Soul can't come back into the Body. In such cases, either the Soul can move on to the higher dimension, or if it gets confused, it might get stuck here because the window to the higher dimension gets closed after 72 hours. We do have many stuck Souls in our dimension.

This is the reason, you may have read in many books or articles, that the number of stuck Souls on earth are more than the total number of people existing on earth. The reason why they may have got stuck may vary. So you see, even at the time of Death, the Soul is playing its dirty games with the Body.

NATURAL DEATH

Natural death is when a person passes away naturally, without suffering from any medical issues or any accidents. One night he goes to bed, and does not wake up in the morning. Mostly, the Soul realizes that it has achieved all what it had planned for in its Macro level plan and now it can leave. So it just decides the date and time and simply leaves the human body. Also, as it was a confident decision, it very easily moves to the other dimension through the 72 hour window, leaving the body here.

Accidental or sudden death–Death in an accident, war, natural calamities. Accidental death, as the name suggests, happens when a person meets with an accident and dies, either on the spot, or within a few minutes or hours of meeting with the accident.

Rarely, this accident could be a part of the Soul Plan.

Mostly, it is not. Therefore, it comes as a shock of a very high intensity to the Soul. As soon as the accident occurs, the Soul goes in a big state of shock because it had not planned for it in the Soul Plan. Also, because the body gets damaged to such an extent that it can't be put back together, the Soul has to move out or get detached from the physical body.

In this case as well, the 72 hour window opens for the Soul so that it can pass through to the higher dimension, however as the Soul is shocked and it still has to accomplish a lot of tasks it had planned in the Soul Plan, it doesn't want to leave. It gets very confused and traumatized. As a result, it doesn't pass through the window and the window gets closed after 72 hours. Now the Soul gets permanently stuck here. By the time, it realizes its mistake, it's already too late.

The same thing happens in case someone is murdered or killed. Unless this was in one's Soul Plan, the Soul gets traumatized, shocked and confused and forgets to pass through to the other dimension.

This Soul keeps wandering around in a traumatized state, looking for a host. Souls need energy to survive in this dimension and they get this energy from a human body. Therefore, there is always a fight or competition between such Souls to get attached to some human body, which may actually be of some other Soul.

Medical - Medical reasons leading to a person's death are mostly planned and are built into the Soul Plan. The medical condition planned by the Soul can be of two types-

a) **Sudden –** examples of such cases include a sudden massive heart attack or a haemorrhage or any other medical emergency which leads to death. This may have been in the Soul Plan or may not. Again, if it was not in the Soul Plan, then the Soul comes into a state of shock and may not pass through, therefore getting stuck here, in this dimension.

b) Prolonged illness – This refers to any kind of prolonged illness which eventually leads to the death of a person. Mostly these are to make the person and his near and dear ones learn some important lessons. E.g. If a wife is suffering from cancer, it may have been planned so that her husband can learn a lesson of caring and giving unconditional love.

Suicide - There may be some questions running in your mind about why do people commit a suicide? Is a suicide also planned before taking birth? Is it a part of the Soul Plan?

In our experience, and the knowledge we have gained so far through our clients, we have not come to know of even a single case where suicide was a part of the Soul Plan.

Souls never really "plan" to end their lives. They do plan situations which are very rough and tough to handle, challenges which are very difficult e.g. difficult relationships, abuse, rape, illness, poverty, financial loss, severe depression etc, however they never ever plan a suicide beforehand. They may however keep suicide as an option, rather a probability if they are just not able to get through the challenging situation at all and they get too overwhelmed.

If the circumstances, which they defined for themselves in the Soul Plan, become too difficult or they get into a complete deadlock kind of a situation, they may have to forcibly take a decision to end their life.

UNEXPLAINED DEATHS - MISCARRIAGE

Many a times, women suffer from miscarriages during the course of pregnancy. In a lot of such cases, what happens is that if a soul realizes that it won't be able to fulfil its life purpose or, it won't be able to learn the lessons it had planned to learn in the next life, by taking birth in this particular family, it leaves the embryo and detaches itself from the embryo and the mother both. This is when the miscarriage happens. The soul leaves this particular family and starts searching for another family where it can take birth.

STILL BIRTH

Many a times, babies are still born without any obvious cause or reason, even after a healthy pregnancy. This is also due to the same reason i.e. the soul may have realized that this family is not the right choice and that it must look out for another family to take birth in, to fulfil its life plan, it may just leave the body during the delivery.

DEATH AFTER TAKING BIRTH

This may also happen in a few days or a couple of years after taking birth.

If the soul gets a feeling that it has taken birth in a wrong family, i.e. it won't be able to fulfil what it had planned for in the next birth in this particular family, it may just leave the body.

Though it is very much dependent upon the baby's soul to take a decision on whether it would continue in the same family or look out for another family, sometimes, still births, miscarriages or death of a baby within 1-2 years of taking birth can also be due to some Karmic lesson that the Souls of the mother, the father or both need to learn.

It may also depend upon the fears or phobias or beliefs the mother, father or both are carrying with respect to giving birth and further on appropriately being able to take care of the child.

REAL LIFE CASE STUDIES - MULTIPLE MISCARRIAGES

This case study is about a couple who had come over to us to get an answer to the multiple miscarriages they had suffered since the time they planned to conceive. Every time in the course of pregnancy, something or the other would happen and they would lose their baby. Once, they even had a stillbirth.

When we regressed the client to find the root cause of the problem, she went back to a time wherein she was a male doctor and was involved in a practice of female feticides to earn huge sums of money. This was the reason, now when she desperately wanted to conceive; she was first not able to conceive. When she was able to conceive, she suffered from miscarriages. When she was able to continue with the pregnancy, she gave birth to a stillborn child.

Here, in the previous lifetime, the Soul wanted to teach a lesson that how painful and what agony a mother has to go through by losing the would be children and not to be a successful mother!

BABY DIED WITHIN 10 DAYS OF TAKING BIRTH

There was a couple who had come to us in a very depressed state, especially the female. Reason was that they had given birth to a beautiful and healthy baby girl. However, within 10 days of taking birth, the girl passed away with no known medical reasons. Some doctors said that it may have happened due to milk going into the respiratory track of the baby, another doctor said something else.

When we did the session, we were able to talk to the soul of that baby girl. When we asked her why did she leave, she told us that she was very sorry about causing the trouble to her parents, however, she realized after 4-5 days of taking birth that this was not the family in which she would be able to meet her goals which she had laid down in her macro level life plan. She needed a family who were not too well off, so that when she grows up, she becomes their support. This was the reason why she had to leave.

The Year-end comes and account has to be closed or squared. We all know about it, still we fear the closure. We leave behind lot of debts & credits, knowing very well that they have to be carried forward to be transferred to next year. Why cannot we plan in advance to square all debts and credits well in advance, before the Year ends? It is our Soul which does not allow us to clear as it will then deviate from its game plan of Karmic creations for next life.

Chapter Seven

Soul Attachments and Fragments Subsidiaries and Ancillary Charges

WHAT IS SOUL ATTACHMENT?

Soul's tyranny does not end at the time of Death, when the Soul has to leave the Body. It has the power to attach to any existing/ live Body. This is a new concept in which we will find out how two or more wayward Souls enter into another living Body.

If we look in terms of Balance sheet, the Soul attachments come under the category of subsidiaries. In a business setting, a subsidiary company is made part of a parent company to assist or supplement it. A parent company owns a foreign subsidiary company, willingly and with full consent to serve its own purpose. In this case, the subsidiary must dutifully follow the laws and interest of the parent company.

But sometimes personal vested interest comes and the subsidiary considers to gain benefits by misusing the parent company. They manage to grow faster than the parent company by copying the technology or enforcing their own and the parent company is left behind struggling to survive.

This is what is happening in Soul attachment, the Body is taken over and controlled by another Soul and in some cases multiple Souls, without its permission or knowledge, hampering even the primary activities of the Body. Since the attached Soul has come to fulfill its own selfish goals, it has no interest in the welfare of the host Body.

The original Soul was given one Body for its own living but then it became greedy and allowed another one to share the same Body. Here comes the theory of subletting the house without taking the permission from the owner- the Body.

The question is when the Soul has been provided single ownership of the house (the Body), why is it inviting others to come and stay? Like any lease agreements, isn't it a breach of contract and responsibility? After doing so, the Soul itself takes the back seat and allows other Souls to take charge of the house, torture the Body to adapt the unwanted habits of the new forced entrants. If the Soul really cared for the Body, it would never have allowed any wayward Soul to enter into it.

For example, if a drunkard's Soul attaches to a person with no such habits, it makes the host Body to get into excessive drinking, leading to loss of money, sickness, poverty and untimely death.

And when this is not enough, at times it invitees in, a hoard of friends (other Souls) and again that too without taking any permission from the Body. Daily party goes on and the house is shattered because of excessive inhabitants and strain on infrastructure. The original occupant- the host Soul does absolutely nothing to stop this exploitation.

HOW DOES A WAYWARD SOUL GET ATTACHED TO THE HOST'S BODY?

We believe that any living or non-living thing has an energy field around it, or a subtle Body which is called an "Aura", which consists of seven levels/layers/auric bodies, also known as the physical, astral, lower, higher, cellular, intuitional, and absolute planes. Each of these bodies has its own unique frequency. They are interrelated, and each Body affects the others. A state of imbalance in one of the Body, leads to imbalance in the others.

When our aura becomes weak, these wayward Souls take advantage of the same and enter in our Body. The reason for this weakness maybe one or many at the same time, say physical illness, trauma, depression or psychological, emotional disturbance, prolonged illness, surgery, accident, loud voice, substance abuse and even during menstrual period.

Certain areas are hot spots for the wayward Souls—

- Hospitals, generally are always carrying lots of lost Souls, who are looking for hosts. So, if someone is in a hospital for surgery, anesthesia can make him/her more vulnerable.
- Temples, Churches, Mosques, Mortuary, cemeteries, pubs, joints.
- Souls do have a tendency to get drawn towards people with a similar tendency.
- Metro and railway stations, airports, and roads may also hold Souls that are 'trying to get home'.

Now, if a person is susceptible and a Soul is able to get through his cracked aura and attach itself to him, what happens to that person?

This person would start putting in all efforts to fulfil a different purpose, which has no correlation with his own goal or purpose in life. The biggest issue is that this happens without any conscious realization or permission from the host's Body. The wayward Souls secretly sneaks into the Body of the Host. Mostly, people have a feeling that they are doing something that they should not be doing, or behaving in a manner in which they should not be behaving, but they don't have any understanding of or control, up to what extent and exactly where they are going wrong.

The wayward Soul acts as a parasite on the human Body and enjoys all the life benefits by being there as it is getting good food, shelter, comfort, fulfilling sexual desires, company and a good luxurious life. It is in no hurry to leave.

Depending on the cause, it can be detected or exhibited immediately, at times may be noticed after a number of years or even may go unnoticed for a lifetime.

DO WAYWARD SOULS HAVE A CHOICE TO EXIT THE HOST'S BODY?

In certain cases, where the wayward Soul has fulfilled all its desires through the Host Body and now has no use of the present Body, but has the knowledge that the window to the other dimension that opened for it has closed already, it may lead the person into committing suicide. This is purely with the selfish perspective that if the Host Body dies, another window will open for it for next 72 hours through which it can piggy back on to the Host Soul and can get on to the other side and get released.

In other cases, Souls themselves get tired of clinging on and get a realization that remaining attached to someone else isn't serving their purpose. In such cases, either the Soul will drag the person to a healer or will create a situation in that person's family which would compel his relatives to bring him to a healer such as a Hypnotherapist for therapy. In certain cases the wayward Souls do frequent in and out too.

Case of a Suicidal, Angry & Aggressive 17 year old girl who preferred dressing up like boys—

During her hypnosis session, she went years back to the time when she was about 5 years old and used to stay somewhere in Delhi.

FINDINGS DURING THE SESSION

She saw her brother who was 2 years old at that time. He was pointing towards something. When she looked towards that side, she saw a teenage boy who was wearing a track pant and a full sleeves shirt, which was properly buttoned. We asked her to initiate a dialogue with him. Initially he refused to talk.

After much perusal, he told her that he has been with her since that time. He also told her that he had met with an accident on the main road next to her house and had died on the spot. Confused and shocked, he ran inside their house's main door and saw her playing in the living room. In a bid to protect himself, he just entered into her aura, which was weak at that time. Since then, he has been dwelling inside her aura.

As the Soul was that of a boy, the girl started developing preference for male dressing.

She became more aggressive and suicidal as she grew up as the Soul of the boy felt trapped and wanted to get released.

SOUL FRAGMENTS

In the balance sheet of Life, the Soul fragments comes under the category of Ancillary charges. Any hidden cost or other expenses involved in a transaction but not directly related to comes under the category of Ancillary Charges.

Have you ever heard statements like, "She is falling apart", "A part of me is missing it seems", "I always seek permission for the smallest activity from my father", "Father had passed away a few years back", "If I don't wear the watch my mother had given me on my birthday, I feel irritated".

All these statements in a way show that a person is carrying an additional baggage, someone is missing a part of oneself or a person feels lost somewhere. These missing links are our or other person's Soul fragments, which get attached without one's knowledge or permission. That is why in accounting language- they are called the Ancillary charges.

The Soul fragment of our dear ones with whom we share a very strong bond of love and affection may get attached. These relationships can be of- mother and child, husband and wife, grandparents and grandchildren, siblings, lovers, friends, teacher, student etc. Sometimes, if you are very attached to some person and they passes away, their soul fragments remain attached to you. This is not just all, your soul fragments may even get attached to a living person if you are too attached to that person.

We not only share our Soul fragments with our loved ones but also with people whom we hate or dislike the most- our enemies, business rivals, competitors, past lovers, in-laws, ex-husbands, ex-wives, bosses, subordinates or colleagues.

Whenever we undergo any kind of trauma or abuse, be it physical or mental, it may just happen that our soul gets fragmented and these fragments get stuck at the place where the event happened, or with people who were present at the time of the event.

The return of the missing fragment of the soul brings with it a new uplifting energy with a new enthusiasm and approach towards life. It has been seen that people start behaving and perceiving things in a more positive manner when their soul becomes whole.

So you see, the tyranny of the Soul does not end at Death. The Soul is capable of harassing the Body through attaching itself to another Body and even through its fragments as well.

A CASE OF A 23 YEAR OLD BOY WITH SUICIDAL TENDENCIES

Sahil had tried to commit suicide again by cutting his wrists... for the third time in his overall life of 23 years.

There was no obvious reason for his behavior as he was intelligent, good looking, had many friends and outgoing. He even had a caring girlfriend if that matters! He couldn't specify any specific point in his life, when he started getting these feelings of committing suicide. For him, there was a constant feeling of sinking since the time he started growing up.

His Hypnotherapy session revealed all together a different point. He went directly to the point in his life where he saw himself as a small baby spending considerable amount of time with his grandmother. She was a doting grandmother and Sahil was the apple of her eyes. They shared a very strong bond of affection. Then the time came when his grandmother passed away. It was an irreconcilable loss for Sahil. He spent days and months crying for her.

This happened when Sahil was only 12 years old. He attempted his first suicide when he was just 14 year old and for no obvious reasons. When we took the boy in trance to that event where his grand mom's Body was being taken to the crematorium, he clearly saw parts of Soul splitting up from his Body and attaching themselves to grandmother's Soul as she was crossing over dimensions and also the Soul fragments of the dead grandmother attaching to Sahil as both of them were very attach to each other, their separation from each other was very difficult. These Soul fragments of Sahil and the grandmother were the actual culprits who were creating havoc in Sahil's life.

Chapter Eight

Fears and Phobias : Taxation Fever

What would you say, if asked, what are Taxes? For general understanding Taxes are compulsory or mandatory financial charges imposed by the government on the general public for the contribution in the State Revenue. For the government, Taxes are the primary source for funding various public expenditures.

Let's us now see what the general public has to say about Taxes- *"We are always worried about the way income tax is applied"*, *"Paying taxes we feel the pinch"*, *for some "It is a real pain and a big fear to comply with"*, *"Taxes are intrusive"* and for some, *"Taxes wore us down"*. So one can say, in general if given a choice we would not like to pay taxes. We all are afraid of taxes and even the thought of paying the taxes makes us uncomfortable.

In the balance sheet of Life, the *Fears* and *Phobias* comes under the category of taxes. The way we get traumatized whenever there is any communication from a Taxation Inspector, same way we get disturbed of these old remembrance of the events that had taken place or we have observed. In the previous chapters we learnt about various Games of the Soul for torturing our Body. The Soul has used every trick and tactic to create havoc in our life.

CASE OF A WOMAN WITH CLAUSTROPHOBIA AND FEAR OF TRAVELLING ALONE

A lady 40 years old had an immense fear of travelling alone and claustrophobia. The problem was so intense that even to go to her office, which was only 3 metro stations from her house, she would take her husband along. Not only this, she would get down at every metro station on the way, with tears rolling down her eyes, take a break of about 5 minutes and then take the next metro.

Due to Claustrophobia, she was not able to use lifts and had to use stairs even if that meant climbing 20 floors.

Her family as well as work life was completely disrupted and had come to a major standstill. She was facing relationship issues due to this with her husband and was not growing professionally too.

When we did her first session, we found that in one of her lives, she was locked and abandoned inside a minivan deep in a forest by her own cousin. She was not given any food or water and was left to suffer. She eventually died after a few days while still trying to struggle and find a way out of that van.

In her second session, we pondered upon her fear of travelling alone. It was again related to a past life, wherein she had shifted to a new city along with her family from a very small town. On her first day of hunting for a job, she lost her way back home completely and ended up being trapped in a storm which lasted many hours.

The feelings and emotions of anxiety, of being separated from her loved ones and even dying were carried forward from that life into this life.

"Hey lets go for a trip in the hills this weekend!" we asked a colleague, about a year ago, to which we got a shocking response *"Are you crazy! I can't even think of going on hills! The mere*

thought of going on hills makes me crazy". When we heard this, we thought it seems she is uninterested and hence making excuses.

We have come across many people, who have a fear or phobia of something or the other e.g. Fear of water, fear of heights, fear of darkness, fear of loud noise. The most common of all of them is "The Fear of Unknown".

How about you? Slow down, take a deep breath in and think about it. Do you have a fear of something? For instance snakes? Spiders? Closed spaces? Crowded places? Fear of Flying? Fear of travelling on road? Fear of Dogs? Fear Of falling? Fear of failure, Fear of success etc.

Well, suffering from some or the other kind of fear is very common. People with such fears simply avoid things which triggers their fear.

The problem becomes bigger when Fears turn into Phobias. When a fear of something results into a physical reaction in a person's body, it is no more called a fear. It is termed as Phobia. E.g. increase in heart rate, increased breathing, excessive perspiration, cold hands and feet etc. Sometimes these phobias are completely irrational and hamper a person's personal as well as professional life to a great extent.

If you take a person to a mountain top, who has a Phobia of Heights, he may even get a panic attack, may get dizzy or start vomiting and collapse. Such is the case of Phobias.

Psychologists would often describe Phobias as fears that become so irrational, illogical and persistent that they are no longer based in reality or to the present.

The mere distinction between Fears and Phobias is that Fear is only a feeling, whereas Phobias lead to actual reactions in our physical Body.

Fears are mostly learnt during childhood, whereas Phobias are supposed to be coming from Past Lives.

Example—There may be a person who has an extreme phobia of knives, even though he has never been hurt by a knife, neither has he seen anybody getting hurt by a knife. Where is this Phobia coming from? Certainly from a past life, wherein some incident must have taken place with a knife.

We once had a client who had a fear of travelling alone. As a result, she would decline so many assignments in which she was supposed to travel to different parts in India as well as overseas. This was impacting her work life as well as family life to a great extent. Her professional growth had completely come to a halt. This was adding lots of anxiety & pressure on her Mind.

If we think about it in greater detail, what is bringing in these fears and phobias within us? It is again our Soul. What is the need for the Soul to carry forward such imprints from our past lives which in reality have got nothing to do with our current life, except creating fears and troubling the human Body? He is acting like a Tax Inspector to create a sense of uneasiness, for this gives him pleasure to see our Body passing through these traumatic situations.

Now, you must be wondering- *"An incidence which may have happened with me in one of my past lives 200 years ago, in which I died by drowning in water, why should I be made slave to that fear of water now? Why should I be frightened by the mere sight of any water body?"*

Based on the Soul Plan, the Soul would carry forward the emotional state and even the phobias from one life to another. There is absolutely no necessity for this. If we talk about Karma, it is still something that a human being owes to another human being, however Phobias are not at all needed to be carried forward.

It seems, the Soul just likes to play games with the human Body for its own fun and entertainment and so does the Tax officer.

Chapter Nine

Body Getting Empowered : Soul Game going for a Toss!

Throughout life we face various challenges, losses, debts and we also earn profits through our good deeds. The Soul (our accountant) is constantly working on the Profit and Loss account of our current life, generating revenue statement of what we have earned, and what we have lost. The aim is to tally the balance sheet accurately.

Is the Soul becoming stronger? The Soul's Games are in full play. The Soul is trying to gain full control over our Body by increasing stresses in our life – We are always neck deep into some or the other problems, be it family, relationships, career, diseases. All this is putting in, a lot of pressure on our Body and the Soul is happily watching the game, playing with our sentiments, emotions and giving physical troubles in the form of diseases, disappointments, fears, phobias, heartbreaks and the list goes on.

It is a tussle between us and the accountant and the Tax Inspector on the data presented in the Balance Sheet. All of us know the reality, still cannot contradict what is given in Black and White. Ultimately this bothering figure wins. The bottom line figure is me, my Body and all the games of the Accountant and the Tax Inspectors goes for a toss.

It is me only who can prove how I have arrived at the actual figure and I am working hard and have worked hard to survive and improve it in the current life. Balance sheets are fudged up figures, so are Soul plans. It is my Micro plan which decides on the actual figures and which the Tax Inspector is not able to detect.

When we talk of destiny, Karma, fears and phobias, we highlight that Soul did so, and so we always remain in one or the other fear. We keep praying for the Soul, keep it always in our good thoughts, and looks after it by going to Astrologers, healers, pilgrimages, religious shrines and pundits for performing rituals for the enlightenment of the Soul, thinking all along that the Soul exclusively belongs to us and it is part of us. The fact is in the next incarnation the Soul will take over a new Body, with altogether a new set of plans.

If the Soul would not have been so naughty and selfish, then we would have been able to concentrate on our physical body in a much better way, we could improve on our prosperity, looked well after our family, career and humanity as a whole. The Balance sheet would match the actual accounts.

The dirty game of Soul has distracted us to always spend time on revenge, wrong deeds and to be totally materialistic. It has made us to even forget about spirituality and involve in competition, how to showdown others, win by scrupulous means, steal, beg, borrow, molest, rape, kill etc. and in the process creating negative Karmas for ourselves and getting stuck in the vicious cycle of Karmas from one lifetime to another.

The Soul is always coxing us to do all the above and feel happy, satisfied and victorious as if its mission is accomplished.

Even the Creator of our universe never envisaged this selfish attitude from the Soul. It is now up to us to let the Soul play more games with us and make us suffer even more in the name of "destiny" or "Karma" or we better gear up and do something about it. It's high time, we wake up and empower ourselves to take back charge of our life from the clutches of Soul!

How the Body can take charge : The Karmic wheel in many cases is taking us back instead of future progress. When a past life ends badly, the law of cause and effect follows us in all our next lives, until the issue is resolved, consciously we do not remember any of our past lives or our past Karmas. We do not even remember the faces or names of people with whom we have created these Karmas. We are not even aware of why we are being tortured, humiliated, insulted or victimized.

How good it would have been if the karmic debts with everybody would have been paid in that very particular life time where the Karmas were created and there is no need to carry forward the Karmic balance and bear the trauma of this life in any other lifetime.

If we are rewarded or punished for whatever good / bad Karmas we have done in the current life, there will be no karmic balance and hence no need of maintaining extensive karmic records of numerous lifetimes. For the Creator also there will be so much less work. We must put a stop to this endless, painful and wasteful loop. Life after life experiences would improve, if the Soul makes better life plans, more prosperous and productive than full of jealousy, hatred etc.

How the Body is fighting this battle in the current scenario : The good news is that through the art of 'Knowing the Unknown' as all information/ past records is available at the subconscious level, we have started decoding it. Through Hypnotherapy, this decoding is giving the humanity to slowly win over the atrocities which the Soul is experimenting on the Body. Days are not far off when the humanity will be able to uplift their physical energies to the level of Soul's metaphysical energies and will be able to function independently without any interference from the Soul.

Scientists have changed the definition of Atoms as the "minutest charged particles" through String Theory. These are no more just Protons, Neutrons or Electrons but vibrating, charged particles called Fermions and Bosons. They are under the process of converting and releasing Fermions (basically the physical form of energy) from their base and making them free like Bosons, which are free floating in the Universe and also represent the Meta Physical form of energy. When that is done, tele-transportation will become a reality and we the material objects will have higher frequencies: may one day even match with the Soul and Mind energies which today are placed under Bosons category. When we achieve this, our Body may not even need the Soul and will be able to survive without it.

We the Body have already found our new homes and have plans to establish our civilization on other planets. We have developed medically to get natural and artificial transplants for our different organs and have extended our lives much beyond to what our Souls have planned. We have worked not only for our betterment but are instrumental in improving the life of Crystals, Plants and Animals.

For Crystals we are releasing them from the clutches of huge, gigantic rocks, breaking them down in smaller pieces so that they can be lovingly and respectably worn by the humans and find place around the neck, wrist, fingers and ankles of beautiful female folks. They adorn these Crystals with all love and affections and value their presence in their life. They also find respect and recognition from the healers, who are using and recommending Crystals as an effective tool for dissipating energy for the betterment of human. Through the use of Crystals, now we are able to tide over all the past life Karmas passed on by some naughty/ selfish Soul.

The Plants are being looked after well by the dedicated team of scientists. There are innumerable advances that have taken place in agriculture. Our scientists now can genetically modify crops by isolating genes associated with undesirable traits such as drought tolerance, higher yield potential and herbicide resistance thus increasing the quality and life of 'Plant Age'.

Herbicides are extensively used in gardening, farming, and landscape turf management. Herbicides destroys specific unwanted plants while leaving desirable vegetation relatively unharmed to maximize crop production by diminishing the development of unwanted plants. Herbicides are also applied in ponds and lakes to aid aquatic plants, in forests to prepare logged areas for replanting, and to golf courses, lawns, parks, and other areas to clear out parasitic growth.

Over the years new technologies such as "Green Development" and "Genetically Modified Crops" have been developed to yield high quality and quantity bumper crops.

Cloning is a beautiful advancement of science as it would foremost prevent the extinction of a species apart from all other benefits. We are now able to produce similar population of bacteria, insects, plants and animals of genetically identical individuals that are of great importance. So far our Scientist have successfully created an exact multiple copy of plants and animals.

Surrogacy is yet another great development through which childless couples who do not have any hopes of becoming parents can now have babies which previously they could not even think about. The reason could be—

- Infertility
- Malformation in Womb
- Single parents
- Homosexual - Gay and Lesbian couple
- Women who cannot go through pregnancy due to numerous health issues, who are focused on their career etc.
- Those who carry past curses and traumatic events.

Similarly, longevity of the Body is increasing due to various other Medical advances such as—

- Artificial Body Parts
- Developments of Tissues in labs
- IVF
- Chemotherapy
- Surgery
- DNA Modifications
- Organ Transplant
- Advance Medicines
- Preservation of stem cells

Birth, disease, old age and death are the four miseries that our Body has to go through. We are already developing ways to counter it and Medical science has reached to such an advancement that we are able to protect our body by harnessing various life threatening bacteria and virus to our advantage.

We have already won over life threatening and disabling diseases like Polio. The day is not far away, when the medical science is able to totally conquer over diseases like cancer, diabetes and AIDS. We are able to increase our immunity and are making a breakthrough by changing and upgrading our DNA. Through latest technologies like IVF we are able to select an egg or sperms where the DNA are more disease free.

Organ transplant and use of the body parts of the healthy or dead body is possible now. Our scientists are working on the process of making transplantation of animal organs into humans and in the process helping hundreds and thousands of people in need of a lifesaving transplant.

New techniques are developing for editing the genes of the donor animals such as pigs to make them most safe and suitable for human- transplantable organs. Once this technique will be fully functional, it would be able to solve the organ shortage crisis and in the process save so many lives.

Due to such advances, we are able to increase our life span. The traditional killer diseases of the elderly, such as pneumonia, influenza and tuberculosis have been controlled too, to a large extent by the Medical advances in the last few decades.

The Soul has now started suffering as it is trapped inside the Body for much longer than it had planned to. There is frustration building up in the Soul and because of this, the Soul is making the human Body suffer more and more. The Soul is able to achieve this by bringing in more fears, stress, unexplained pains and aches. Each and every cell of the Body is being made to face the aftermath of all the bad Karmas, negative emotions, habits and actions that have been inculcated by the Soul.

As Einstein said—"it will take a higher level of consciousness to solve the problems we are experiencing than the level of consciousness that created them."

It is time to wake up and evolve our ways of thinking, being and doing. It is time to look inside ourselves and take responsibility for who we are, how we think and what we do. The time is NOW and there is not a spare second to waste.

The Soul Plan, which we all know as our predefined destiny, can now be changed with the power of our "free will". We can create our own destiny and yes we can change our Soul's Macro as well as Micro Level Plans by utilizing the power of our Body. We can conquer the Soul by taking charge of life and manifesting what we want in life and working towards achieving it.

How to take charge of our Body? We can control the Soul from imparting further damages to us and take charge of our Body by:

By doing good Karmas : According to Jainism, Karma is considered to be like a subtle matter or particles or a flowing mass of energy which enters a living body with each activity of the later and envelops it in dark gloom. Karma binds the soul to the matter and makes its liberation an increasingly difficult task. The nature of this substance depends upon the actions performed.

> **"Karma is the root of birth and death. The souls bound by Karma go round and round in the cycle of existence."**

Liberation is possible only when the entry of further Karmic material is blocked by individual efforts, which involve good conduct and non-injury to others.

Our Karmas are what have defined our destiny and it is our Karmas only, which can redefine it! That's the simple rule. Hence, if we keep doing good Karmas, our destiny keeps forming that way. Good Karmas can lead us to go through the same negative event, but less harshly as it was supposed to be according to our Soul plan.

By accessing and making use of our Subconscious Mind : Our Subconscious Mind is extremely powerful. We hardly make any use of it. It is our subconscious Mind on behest of the Soul, makes us feel, behave and perceive things in a particular manner based on our past events. A lot of "how I think, act and perceive" and "how my situations are shaping up" in life, comes from my past. Gautam Buddha also says-

"Our life is the creation of our Mind. Life becomes what the Soul has fed into our Mind."

By healing through Hypnotherapy : With the help of Hypnotherapy, which is a well-defined science emanating from and beyond Psychology, we are able to reach the event, which is creating trouble, heal that event and nullifying that event from our Subconscious Mind. We even nullify the effect it has on us, thus enabling us to create a new feeling, a new perception and therefore a new reality in our physical space. Hence, our past life is worked upon. We regress to the time, when the event happened which caused, "what I am going through today".

When the healing happens, not only our behavior changes, even our physical reality changes. This not only means changes in our situation, but also in our physical Body, thoughts, emotions and surroundings.

By sending out "Good Thoughts" into the universe : When we send out positive thoughts, our Brain leads to the secretion of good hormones or happy hormones in our Body such as Dopamine, Serotonin, Oxytocin, Endorphins, Estrogen, Progesterone, Acetocin etc.

It has been observed that negative thoughts have a much higher frequency than positive thoughts. Similarly, thoughts of anger and fear have a very high frequency.

Hence we need to check our thought process and keep it under strict control and by doing so we are able to prevent miscommunication with the universe.

Paolo Coelho in his famous book *The Alchemist* has said "And, when you want something, all the universe conspires in helping you to achieve it."

By Paying Gratitude : Paying gratitude to the universe for providing whatever was considered appropriate for us. This is a very crucial step. Being grateful for what we have received make us more grateful.

By "Going into the Future" : As much instigating it sounds, it is indeed extremely helpful. In certain cases, when a person is at logger heads with his current life and does not see any hope of betterment we the Hypnotherapists show him the parallel lives. The life that he is living and a few years beyond, and then the other alternate life that is waiting or is available for him if he chooses to adopt. This is like two sides of a coin.

Looking and comparing the pros and cons, he can choose and decide if, is he really at logger heads with current life or is it his own thoughts that are making him think so.

By Meditating : Meditation is a science. Through meditation, the flow of energy in our Body gets restored and regulated. It helps in making our Aura strong. Meditation also leads to the secretion of Happy Hormones, reduce stress, relieve chronic pains, eases out anxiety, increases focus and concentration, strengthens the immune system, enhances emotional & mental wellness and brings in peace and feelings of gratitude.

And the good news is that you can meditate anywhere and anytime, while waking, sitting, playing etc.

By accepting Death as a natural process : All the mythologies say that whosoever takes birth has to end that life. The end of life is called Death. Dying is also an important part of life, because it makes us closer to our ultimate goal which is to grow spiritually and become one with the Creator. Everyone has taken birth to play a role, to fulfil certain task and then finally moving on so that we can play more roles and finish more incomplete tasks. Hence we should learn to accept Death as one of the most crucial parts of human life. We should be happy as our Body is released of trauma so created by the Soul games.

We Humans are also becoming smarter and each day coming up with a new solution to protect and prevent ourselves against all the tortures that the Soul has been imparting on us.

The day is not far when for its existence, the Body may not even need a Soul! Then the Soul energies will have to think about their existence. Body that is me who is experiencing all the trauma, problems, and atrocities at the hands of Soul will be able to totally disconnect from the past life Karmas, by doing so, putting further stop on building more Karmas.

With our free will we can decide not to take revenge and give forgiveness and move forward. What we do in the current life, we are able to close that and do not keep any karmic settlement for the next life. That day is not far when the Body will be able to take charge of its life and be able to totally protect and save itself from further exploitation.

The Soul better take it as a final warning or the last call to mend its ways.

"na jayate mriyate va kadacin 'nayam bhutva bhavita va na bhuyah 'ajo nityah sasvato yam purano 'na hanyate hanyamane sarire..."

(Bhagavad Gita 2.20)

Here Lord Krishna describes the Soul in the following way :

For the soul there is neither birth nor death at any time. He has not come into being, does not come into being, and will not come into being. He is unborn, eternal, ever – existing and primeval. He is not slain when the body is slain.

THIS MAY BECOME A THING OF THE PAST

There have been various sessions on Life between Lives with clients and we conclude this book by sharing one of the classic experience of one of our client's Life between Lives session. This session had a very dramatic end, where our client saw her Soul waiting for her turn to return back on Earth. She saw her Soul standing in front of the Council of Ministers, listening to their instructions, about what all the soul has to do once back on Earth.

She also shared with us their concerns and future plans about Planet Earth. The main concern the Council of Minsters shared- When sent on Earth, the Soul is spending too much time on Karmic Wheel, in the process, using the Body in doing too much of unproductive work and thus wasting and spoiling lots of useful resources of the Earth. This is putting too much pressure on Earth which is already over loaded and overburdened. The natural resources of the Earth are on the verge of depletion. They were worried that the time of Planet Earth is already limited. Soon that time will also come when the Earth will disintegrate and disappear in oblivion.

They also informed her that the Karma theory or karmic wheel was not there at the time of evolution of the universe. It was introduced much later to the Soul to bring understanding, growth, development, love and peace but since the Soul is misusing Karmic wheel, so it is going on a negative slant.

She further described that now the universe is also working on many dimensions to control all this and is in the process of introducing many new concepts—

- The Soul will have memories of its previous lifetimes, will have the capacity and capability to rectify its karmic patterns on its own, and so henceforth need not bother the Human Body to correct them.
- The Human Body once free from the Soul's karmic wheel, will be able to spend its lifetime on Earth in other productive things such as growth and development of mankind, plants, animals, forests, mountains, oceans and other natural resources of the Earth.
- The Humans will learn to connect with other Planets and parts of the Universe by exchanging knowledge and building friendship because there will come a time, when the planet Earth will vanish as it has vanished before, then they will have a place in the Universe to survive.
- The humans will travel across time and space in the Universe. They will be able to control the Soul and their physical bodies both. A movement will come when Humans will be able to put their Soul in a bottle and lock their aura and control the aging and self-degenerating process of the Body. For time travel they will also know how to leave behind their physical body which otherwise would get lost in the gravitational pull of the Universe.

So let's rejoice - that day, which is not far behind when we will be able to capture our Soul or consciousness in a bottle if it is creating too much mess in our current life and neatly put the bottle on a table and decide at leisure–"What to do with it?"

For now we can confidently say—

"Yes! The Soul Game is going for a 'Toss'!"

❑❑

Author's Introduction

Richa Agarwal

- Life & Leadership Coach, Coach For Life Institute, USA
- Counsellor & Corporate Trainer (Employee Development & Wellness)
- Clinical Hypnotherapist, California Hypnosis Institute, USA
- Trainer of Hypnotherapy, California Hypnosis Institute, USA
- Award Winning Screenplay Writer
- Award Winning Film Maker
- Founder : MindSpring -An Alternate Healing & Research Center
- Founder : EpicStar Productions
- Director Culture & Wellness : International Business Chamber Of Commerce

Expertise

- Counselling & Stress Management
- Executive Coaching
- Women Empowerment

- Relationship & Conflict Management
- Leadership Skills Enhancement
- Sports Performance Enhancement
- Behaviour Modification

Member

- American Hypnosis Association
- International Medical & Dental Hypnotherapy Association
- National Guild of Hypnotists
- Hypnosis Motivation Institute
- Script Writers Association of India

Richa holds a Masters Degree in Computer Science and prior to dedicating her life for the betterment of society had a promising career of more than a decade in the software industry. As a Program Management professional, she worked with top multinational corporations heading large scale projects across the world prior to becoming a Corporate Coach. She works with individuals and organisations help realise their dreams in personal and professional lives. She has been conducting workshops for almost a decade now based on subjects like Stress Management, Performance Enhancement, Leaderships Skills Enhancement, Overcome Fears, Anxieties and Phobias etc. in Corporates, Educational Institutions and Hospitals.

In her decade long devotion as a coach, therapist, mentor, guide and counsellor, she has trained more than 2000 employees across organizations; worked with many terminally ill patients and helped them heal at a physical & emotional level; as well as worked with rescued and autistic children.

Her creative side has led her into making a few short films based on the story of her actual clients, first one being "Raaya", based on the story of an autistic girl who showed significant improvement through her therapeutic intervention. She made this film to create awareness in the society about the success of Hypnotherapy in treating Autism. The film won 15 accolades all over the world. It was screened at the "Cannes Film Festival" and won India's most prestigious "Dadasaheb Phalke" award. For her second movie "Khushi" again based on one of her real case, she got the Best Screenplay Writer award at the Delhi International Shorts Film Festival 2019. The movie was also selected for screening at the Dadasaheb Phalke film festival.

Her venture Mindspring is an alternate healing and research center that believes in curing the world of traumas, physiological and psychological afflictions with a wide range of therapies and highly individualized treatments, standalone as well as alongside conventional medical procedures.

Dr. Sunil Prakash

M.B.A, H. B., C.C.Ht., P.L.T, R.Ht. Sunil is a Certified Clinical Hypnotherapist and Certified. Trainer of Clinical Hypnotherapy from California Hypnosis Institute (CHI) a USA, International Medical & Dental Hypnotherapy Association (IMDHA), International Association of Counsellors & Therapist (TACT) -USA, Hypnosis Motivation Institute (HMI) -USA, National Hypnotist Guild (NGH) USA and registered with IBAM, Kolkata. He has been successful running a Hypnotherapy school in India- California Hypnosis Institute Gurgaon, since 2009.

Sunil started his career in 1974 with a large business organization heading the MIS department and moved subsequently into promoting Indian Handicrafts overseas. Since 1990 he has been successfully running his export company.

In 2008 he had a chance meeting with a Clinical Hypnotherapist who introduced him to the effectiveness of Hypnotherapy as a healing modality. Atthat time in India, Hypnotherapy was not a popular healing modality. There were lots of myths and misconceptions linked with Hypnosis.

Sunil got his universal calling to propagate and spread this knowledge. He completed his Hypnotherapist course as well as Trainer's program in less than a year and started practicing and teaching Clinical Hypnotherapy from 2009 onward.

Sunil is the CEO of California Hypnosis Institute Gurgaon. He is a trainer, consultant and therapist to various corporates, institutions and individuals for career planning, sports performance, memory enhancement, self-empowerment, psychosomatic issues such as stress, anger, anxiety, fears, phobias, substance abuse, relationship and marital issues etc.

In his zest to payback society and to make a positive difference in people's lives, Mr. Sunil Prakash has been an active member of various welfare organizations such as Lions Club International and Rotary International, working on various social issues such as leprosy, consumer movement, menstrual hygiene, child and women development and empowering them through skill development, computer and vocational training, and more.